RUNWAYS AND HIGH HEELS AND MURDER

Book Nine: The Fiona Fleming Cozy Mysteries

PATTI LARSEN

Cover design by Christina Gaudet
www.castlekeepcreations.com

Thanks, Kirstin!

ISBN-13: 978-1-988700-93-9

CHAPTER ONE

I had no idea hitting someone could be so emotionally satisfying. Not that I condoned violence on a regular basis, but I did happen to be known for my temper. Still, I usually took the pacifist route on the outside, if I tended to boil over on the inside. This opportunity to actually use my fists to strike out at another human being had much more appeal than I should have allowed myself. And the tight grin and panting half-hiccup, half-giggle that escaped me every time I punched Matt honestly had to go.

Self-defense class was *fun*, yo.

I wasn't sure the park ranger and current love interest of our local deputy-turned-teacher knew what he was getting himself into when Jill Wagner agreed to show a few of the local ladies a thing or two about protecting ourselves. Not that the cutest town in America was all that dangerous or anything, but Reading had its share of visitors from out of town these days with tourism booming as it had been thanks to our mayor's continuing efforts. Oh, and the murders. Yeah. Those. All eight of which I'd had up close and personals with over the last two years.

"That's it, Fee." Matt was doing his best to stay chipper as I whacked him in the ribs with my elbow like Jill taught me. He sounded less than delighted by the solid blow I landed while I snorted my delight at the sheer excitement of letting out some physical tension in a perfectly legal and condoned fashion. Especially since there were other physical tensions building in my life, namely concerning a certain sheriff of said cutest American town and the fact Crew Turner made my madly beating heart go pitter-pat far too often.

I landed another blow before stepping aside, catching Matt's wince, his forced smile as Alicia Conway bounced into my place, her long ponytail bobbing behind her, tiny body surprisingly muscular in her capris and sports tank. I grudgingly gave way to her, almost laughing out loud at the look on Matt's face.

Yup, he was definitely regretting volunteering to be a punching bag.

"Fee, you can join us over here." I followed Jill's direction, quickly crossing the Reading High School gym to her side where she had the group of women not beating the crap out of her boyfriend split into pairs. I'm positive she wasn't expecting our conversation over coffee, joined by my bestie, Daisy Bruce, my mother, Lucy, and the excitable Alicia to spiral out from a couple of ladies learning a move or two from our favorite deputy to what felt like the bulk of the female population in our little town coming out to fill the gym with eager excitement. I'd never seen so much spandex and shelf-bra tank tops in one place in my life and was sure some of the older ladies had pulled out their favorite workout gear from the 80s just for this event.

"Where do you want me?" I knew I was grinning, couldn't help it. Jill seemed a bit frazzled but had taken everything in stride when Alicia turned our group of students into a giant show that required the rental of the gym we stood in. Of course, the fact Olivia Walker was here meant we likely had the place for free. Alicia's frowning suggestion we charge at the door was denied by the deputy's matching frown and now I wondered, looking around at all those women if Jill might be regretting her decision to give up her Saturday morning without compensation.

Oh, Fee. Always the businesswoman.

Jill gestured toward the group and a small selection of women standing off to one side, Mom among them. "You can take a break," she said, "or find a partner and practice some of your blocks."

I saluted with a saucy toss of my head and bounced to my mother who beamed at me, her own trim form neatly dressed in a matching velvet tracksuit with the tightest t-shirt I'd ever seen Mom wear proclaiming her a "Goddess". I think I bought it for her last Christmas and grinned to see her wearing it. She grasped for my hand, tugging me to her side, almost vibrating and a bit breathless.

"How fun is this?" She giggled behind one hand. "Now I know why boys like it so much. It's rather satisfying to just let loose every once in a while, isn't it?"

I didn't remind her this was meant to be protection training, just in case, and instead let her have her entertainment. As far as I was concerned, nothing bad would ever touch my mother, not for as long as my dad had her back. The big, retired sheriff might have been working as a P.I. these days, but that didn't mean my father was a slouch at making sure Mom was safe and secure.

Still, the niggling worries about their past, his, in particular tied to the mysterious Siobhan Doyle and local Irish mafia boss, Malcolm Murray, lingered like a toothache I just couldn't shake. You'd think making me a partner in Fleming Investigations without my consent or knowledge would mean Dad would be open to sharing what he knew about the mess I seemed only able to uncover in drips and bits. But no, not John Fleming. I might as well ask for him to hand over his gun and his will to live.

Mom glanced at Matt just as Alicia landed a particularly sharp blow to his already abused ribs and actually winced. "Poor boy," she said, though I'd seen her take her own gleeful shots at him just a few minutes ago. "You should have asked Crew to come and help out so Matt wouldn't have to do this alone."

I laughed. "I did." Did I. And was turned down as he broke into an almost hysterical laugh of his own. "He said he's had enough of being a target of the women in Reading."

Mom snorted delicately, green eyes that matched mine sparkly. "Point taken. Still, he must be happy you decided to do this. What with all the troubles."

My mother's polite way of saying she worried about me and was grateful to know I might actually be able to defend myself if something happened. Because, just my luck, something would again, wouldn't it? "Him and Dad and you and Daisy and everyone else I talked to," I found myself grumbling.

"We just want you to be safe, Fee," Mom said, patting my arm. "If you'd stop finding dead bodies and almost dying on us, maybe we'd stop worrying."

What had she said? Point taken? Grumble.

Daisy bounded to my side, her own dark blonde hair in two plaited braids, looking adorable in her trendy workout clothes. She'd returned from her father's funeral a different woman, though not in the way I'd feared. When she'd gone to Montpelier with her half-sister, Rose Norton, back in November, I'd been sure the time together would turn into a disaster for her. Since I was positive it was Rose who influenced Daisy and made her doubt herself in the first place, I'd fully expected my bestie would be completely lost to me when she came home again. If she even came back at all, partnership or not. I'd been witness firsthand to the influence Rose had on

Day, as had Mom. Which was why we were both shocked and delighted the morning Daisy rolled in, gray eyes sad but lips smiling, and firmly and cheerfully took her place yet again as part of our combined business.

There wasn't much said, and I didn't press her, though Rose seemed put out and unhappy by the whole attitude Daisy wore. Which meant I was delighted, naturally. If what happened between them was something my best friend felt the need to share with me down the road, I'd be here for her. I was just happy the stressful clashing we'd done over the last year—all thanks to Rose, I had no qualms saying it in my head or out loud—was done and buried.

I'd hoped the change in their relationship would mean Rose would wander off back to Montpelier and stay there. No such luck. Wouldn't you know her little love affair—gag, barf, kill it with fire—with my cousin, Robert Carlisle, meant she was staying put for as long as the two of them were in—choke, wheeze, gross—love.

Dear god, please don't let them breed.

One of my most satisfying moments was watching Rose flounce in that morning, realize she actually had to do some work, and flounce out again, leaving the rest of us to enjoy ourselves. From the way the other women seemed equally happy to see her go, it was clear Rose wasn't making friends in Reading and I hoped the tide had turned permanently against Robert, too. Sure, he was technically related to us—an accident of birth I longed for the means to rectify—he wasn't a Fleming no matter how much some townsfolk wished that were true. His pompous nature and the way he'd fallen down on the job, along with Olivia's resurgence in popularity—and Crew's along with her—had created a definitely lean toward Rosebert being on the outs and, thanks to Dad's thriving P.I. business, even more reliance on my family than ever.

At least Crew wasn't being punished for it any longer. That he was telling me about.

I waved at Olivia who was actually sweating, her shining dark bob tucked back behind her ears. She actually looked human and like she was enjoying herself as she sparred with Vivian French. I'd been thinking a lot lately about the Queen of Wheat. Had mostly dropped my animosity toward her, thanks to her support of my mother, her show of humanity from time to time. If Mom trusted her, I'd give her the benefit of the doubt despite our past. But her obvious connection to the Patterson family and her influence over town council had been made pretty apparent in the debates of the fall, something I still hadn't come to grips with. And no number of attempts to corner her or invite her for coffee had gained me even an inch of ground on the subject.

I had a love/hate relationship with mysteries that I honestly wasn't sure if I could live without. Good thing Reading had no end of things for me to poke my nose into then, wasn't it?

As I stepped back and looked around, I had this sudden surge of pride hit me almost like a blow. Talk about girl power. I grew up in Reading, left for ten years, and came home to slide into my Grandmother Iris's comfortable if well-worn shoes. And while I'd come to think of Reading as the place I wanted to spend the rest of my life, this was the first time I felt such a powerful kinship with my Reading sisterhood. I was grinning again, hugged Mom around the shoulders, my heart full and my head clear.

All was right in the world, or at least my small corner of it.

What was it about actually thinking such things that ensured disaster was just around the corner? Pessimist. Who, me?

CHAPTER TWO

"Fee, can I talk to you a moment?"

I hadn't seen much of Alice Moore the last few months, but that didn't mean much. Life was so busy, running into old acquaintances I considered friends happened less frequently than expected, even in such a small town as Reading. The young, self-proclaimed medium looked great, happier than ever, her slightly-on-the-skinny-side body looking more muscular than emaciated these days, her beaming smile at least boding well for the nature of her requested conversation. I felt tension leave me when I registered her upbeat mood and nodded a welcome, wondering what had gotten into me that a polite request to chat put my back up at all.

Sheesh, Fee. Not every talk had to be bad news.

Alice stood next to me, her dark hair in a ponytail halfway down her back, her big, almost haunting hazel eyes watching me with that kind of creepy focus I was used to when it came to her. She'd gotten herself contacts at some point since I saw her last, making her gaze even more intense, usually hidden behind the thick lenses of her glasses. I'd once called her plain in my head, felt guilty about labeling her by her looks rather than her personality, and realized I was wrong. Maybe it was love—she and Denver Hatch, grandson of the deceased fake psychic who'd brought us all together, were still a couple as far as I knew—or her attitude, but the mid-twentysomething young woman with the thin, pale face and intent attention when she looked at you was far prettier these days than I'd given her credit for.

Not that looks were important. Fee, seriously.

"Nice to see you, Alice." I felt my cheeks heat from my line of thought and hoped she'd chalk it up to the workout. "How's Denver?"

It was her turn to flush, slow blinks of her long lashes answering that question. "He's wonderful," she said. Not gushing, because Alice didn't. But about as close to it as she was going to get in her soft voice. "He says hello."

"What can I do for you?" I grinned at Daisy who took her turn whacking Matt. She had a wicked left hook I hadn't noticed before. Mind you, she'd never hit me, had she?

"I was hoping I could ask your advice." Alice hesitated before rushing on while my mind whirled about what she might possibly ask me to help her with. "I've been taking on a few jobs out of state lately. Denver's been coming with me. We've started a paranormal investigation company. A bit more official than my blog." She cleared her throat, her jagged sentences sounding stiff and well-orchestrated, too much so to be random. So, she'd thought ahead about what she was going to say? Was I that intimidating to my friends or was it just Alice? "While I've made a good living from advertising on my page, Denver thought it might be a great idea to actually make the business official." She blinked slowly again, paused. Waited. For what? My approval? I nodded slowly, so confused but pretty sure she was going to get to the point and willing to wait her out, though I didn't afford that kind of patience to many people. Alice was different. Like creepily awesome different. She grinned when I nodded as if I'd done her a huge favor and went on, talking faster now. "I was hoping I might be able to call on you from time to time, just in case I run into something I can't handle. Or need to bounce ideas off someone."

Whoa. Wait a second. "You're pursuing murder investigations?" Dad would be a better choice.

But Alice looked startled then amused. "Not the way you think," she said, laughter in her voice. "Though there will be death involved, we'll be looking into the kinds of cases that include hauntings, not necessarily uncovering murderers." Her lips twitched as she sighed. "It's just that I have to deal with the living, you know? I'm so much better at handling the dead."

Yeah, that wasn't freaky or anything, Alice. I had to admit, I was intrigued, and more than a bit creeped out. After all, I still didn't have a solid explanation for the ghost sighting of Manuel Cortez two Halloween's ago, the night Sadie Hatch was murdered by that same young man's father. Alice's forte wasn't mine, her pursuit of debunking hauntings and those who used them for their own gain much more macabre than running a B&B.

Okay, who was I kidding? I was up to, what, eight dead bodies at this point? Knowing my face had to register wry amusement, I shrugged.

"If you think I can ever be of help," I said, "feel free."

She seemed relieved by the offer and hugged me suddenly, surprisingly, before she stepped away, her own face startled like I'd been the one to instigate the embrace. She rubbed both thin hands together, the lingering chill of their touch on my back making me shiver. But she was still smiling and bobbed a final nod before turning and walking away, joining a group of women standing around Jill.

I was about to follow her when Alicia bounded up to me, grinning. "Great class!" She seemed about as wound up as ever, and maybe even more so, ready if the little fists she held at both her sides were any indication, ready to test out her newfound abilities on Jared Wilkins, her fiancé when she got home.

"Awesome." I beamed at her, doing my best to

avoid the tiny knot of hurt that lingered between us. "How are the wedding plans coming along?"

Her face fell slightly, her expression turning from open happy to guarded in a flash that told me I shouldn't have opened my big mouth. When she and Jared informed me just a few weeks ago they had to cancel their plans to use the annex for their wedding, that family pressure had led them to instead use the Marie Patterson Equestrian Center, I'd done my best not to let my young friends see my disappointment. It wasn't their fault the Pattersons seemed to get everything they wanted, even with Jared's mother, Aundrea, formerly on the outs. Maybe things had changed. If so, though, I hoped it didn't mean the end of my friendships with the young couple. I adored them both too much to lose them over something as dumb as hurt feelings about a wedding venue.

"Fine," Alicia said, fake smile flashing, eyes sad before she bounded away again.

Well, crappy. That would be the last time I asked. I'd stayed out of it, including asking Aundrea herself, the happily married woman in question beaming at her wife as she and Pamela Shard joined the others watching Jill. But my nosiness hadn't kept me from asking the newspaperwoman her opinion the day after Alicia and Jared came to tell me the news.

I'd expected something from Pamela. Some kind of snarky comeback about the Pattersons, some reaction in accordance with the hard-nosed former *Boston Globe* photojournalist. Instead, she'd shrugged and refused to answer, practically ushering me out of her office and closing the door behind her.

Okay, so I was standing here now in the gym weeks later, glaring at Pamela as I remembered her reticence to talk. And, come to think of it, she'd been sort of avoiding me lately, hadn't she? Despite my continuing column contributions to the *Reading Reader Gazette*. Hadn't her own stories become rather tame lately? Compared to how scathing they used to be, tearing Olivia a new one on a regular basis, even going after Crew and the Patterson family. I'd noted since the wedding she'd started easing up on all of them, as if someone—one guess as to who—was pressuring her to stop rocking the Reading boat.

There were times I'd had it up to here with Marie Patterson and the matriarch of the founding family's interference with the people I cared about. The image of a bloated, grinning spider pulling threads of a web she'd woven over the town I'd come to love despite hating it as a child made my blood boil. But what was I going to do about it?

I was scowling, could feel it tugging at my mouth, forming a line between my brows. Well, I could do something. I could write more scathing columns myself, right? If Pamela wasn't willing to do it...

And then it hit me, like a ton of bricks it struck me so hard I gasped, gaining Mom's attention and her own frown of concern before I shook my head and caught myself instead grinning this time.

Clever, that Pamela Shard. Because that was likely her point, wasn't it? She wasn't able to write the stories she wanted. And knew the softer she became, the harsher I'd be. Okay, so I could have been wrong, but I really doubted it. Like I needed another job, with Petunia's and the annex and Fleming Investigations... then again, spring was quiet, right? And Dad wasn't super busy just then. So, I had time to dig in a bit and see what kind of mischief I could create.

One thing was certain, I'd have my answer soon enough. Because if Pamela refused to publish what I wrote, she really had gone soft and the Pattersons had gotten to her. But if she shared what I gave her...?

Well. We'd just see what it took to make Marie Patterson sit up and take notice.

CHAPTER THREE

I joined Mom as she looked up from smiling at something Vivian had said, my insides crawling just a little at the sight. Okay, so I didn't have the same animosity toward the Queen of Wheat I used to—I was mostly over the bullying she'd done to Daisy that ended in me breaking her nose when we were kids, wasn't I?—but there was a part of me that still mistrusted and disliked her. But was it on principle or based in fact? She'd proven herself loyal to the status quo as far as I was concerned and while that wasn't exactly a bad thing, considering my own support of Olivia, which could be construed as the same type of attachment, I knew understanding why I still didn't name Vivian among my peeps would require a long, hard look inside. A journey I wasn't sure I was ready to take.

Clinging to the past, who, me?

"Fee." Mom never seemed to care that my reticence lingered, pulling me by the hand into their circle and the conversation with her own breathless excitement making me nervous. "Vivian asked me to assist with the catering for the fashion show this week. Isn't that amazing?"

I'd vowed to stay out of other people's business—at least the actual running of registered companies if not their activities I might find suspicious or intriguing—since last fall and the whole Black Mountain fiasco. I was done helping others, but it seemed Mom wasn't of the same mind as me. She continued to try to drag me into assisting her in her catering efforts and while I hated to say no, I'd been doing so all winter.

But something about the tight, expectant look in Vivian's icy blue eyes triggered my generosity, if only because I thought I knew what she was thinking. That Fiona Fleming would never step up to help her. The twinge of annoyance that she might even suggest she knew my mind set off a chain of thought processes that ended with me smiling at Mom in a stiff and rather formal way as I opened my big mouth and spoke.

"Happy to assist," I said while my mother squealed and hugged me. "Anything I can do."

Dear god, what was wrong with me? Had I really just volunteered to help Vivian French without her having to say a freaking word? That long, hard look inside? Yeah, I'd be dealing with that immediately because there was no way I was spending another second or another ounce of energy caring what Vivian thought.

"Thank you, Fee." At least she sounded gracious, even if her expression never changed while Mom's beaming smile made up for the deficit. "I realize you're busy."

Wow, that was actually thoughtful. Huh. "No problem," I said. "Spring's a bit quieter, so I have time." Way to go, Fleming, being all professional and polite.

Vivian nodded, stiff and formal, but I was sure she seemed to relax just a bit as she spoke again, this time to Mom directly, warmth returning to her voice. "I appreciate your assistance, Lucy," she said, not even trying to keep her voice down. "The quality of catering I require is, unfortunately, above the present staff at the White Valley Lodge." I caught Alicia's flinch, but the young manager of the local hotel didn't march her butt over and tell Vivian off. Quite to the contrary. Alicia instead seemed embarrassed and hustled out of earshot.

I tried not to gape at Vivian for her obvious slur against my friend but didn't get to say anything in Alicia's defense as Mom responded.

"I'm sure that's not the case." Leave it to Lucy Fleming and her retired principal attitude to strike exactly the right chord of chastisement mixed with reassurance. Vivian just shrugged her narrow shoulders inside her designer workout tank.

"With Chef Chaney's departure, you were the obvious choice." I hadn't realized Carol had quit. Interesting, but people moved on all the time. I'd had zero interaction with her outside of the occasional run-in at Sammy's Coffee since the stormy weekend Mason Patterson died from a slice of chocolate cake. I'd always liked her, even if I didn't know her well, and hoped she'd moved on to greener pastures. I did glance Alicia's way, wondering at the story behind the loss of the chef, though, and if the young manager was in some kind of trouble. I'd done my best to be there for her and Jared, sent all of my guests to *Zip It!*, his co-owned zipline park. I realized then the distance between us hadn't been sudden or due to the wedding's relocation but had been going on for some time and a soft wave of sadness hit me harder than I was expecting.

I could only imagine it had to do with me and that only made things worse. Blinking away the sting of impending tears before they could gather, I instead chose to focus on Mom while asking myself a hard question—was writing my column and prodding the Patterson family really worth losing my friends over? Or was that the source of their distance after all?

"This is an amazing opportunity," Vivian was saying, long, pale hair sliding over her bare arm as she tossed her head. "I can't wait to see the designs coming this season. Having a chance to preview them in a personal venue is unheard of."

I had zero experience with the fashion world outside of Fashion Week in New York. I'd lived there long enough I knew to avoid certain streets at certain times of the day. And the city was filled with wannabe models working as baristas and servers and cashiers, so it wasn't like I didn't know a few in my time living in the Big Apple. For some reason, Vivian seemed much more in the know and I wondered suddenly how she'd managed to pull off this event in the first place. She owned a string of bakeries, not a clothing store line.

"I'm so excited," Mom gushed at her. "I've never been to a real fashion show before."

Vivian's smile seemed genuine enough. Was that a hint of sadness behind her expression, though? "I think you'll enjoy it, Lucy." She glanced at her watch. "Now, if you'll excuse me, I have to go pick up Grace at the airport." Vivian turned to me, stiff all over again. Seemed like I wasn't the only one with buried issues to deal with. "I've emailed you the list of guests I'm sending you," she said. "Daisy confirmed but I wanted to be sure you received it personally." There had been a few instances of reservations going missing and parties being scheduled incorrectly on my bestie's watch the last six months, but I still resented Vivian's implication.

"Everything's ready," I said, knowing I sounded as stilted and formal as she did. "The annex is at your disposal." Sheesh, Fee, were we in an old literary novel or something?

"Grace Fiore is a very special guest, Fee," Vivian said like I didn't treat all of my guests like they were valuable to me. "I want assurances she'll have a pleasant and positive stay in Reading. That is if we ever hope to have something like this held here again."

She actually sounded like she cared what this woman thought. Wait, wasn't that the name of the designer Vivian always wore? Yes, I was sure of it, had heard her mention her before. Were they friends or was Vivian sucking up to an idol?

Didn't matter to me, not a bit. Right?

"I'll do my best," I said. "She's not the first celebrity I've housed, Vivian."

I had to bring that up, didn't I? Vivian's face tightened further as my mind flinched from the memory of Willow Pink and Skip Anderson, the former, while famous and lovely, widowed from the latter when he died in my lap. Whoops. Not exactly reassuring.

Mom leaped in with a hand on Vivian's arm. "I can't wait to meet her," she said, with just the right amount of reverence, apparently, because the pale blonde smiled instead of snapping my head off. "So wonderful of her to come to Reading like this. You must be dear friends."

Vivian's faint nod answered the personal question, but her words were crisp. "Olivia has made it financially appealing," she said. "The six designers we're expecting will give us an amazing show, I'm sure." Pretty easy to tell from her snotty tone which of the six she expected to shine the brightest. And now I was anticipating the guest from hell in Grace Fiore. Awesome.

As long as the cameras and drama steered clear of Petunia's, I could bury myself in work and keep out of the whole deal until it was all over. Oh, wait. I'd just volunteered to help, hadn't I?

Sigh.

"I assume I can count on your discretion." Vivian closed the distance between us, voice dropping at last. "Grace prefers to stay outside the main venue for privacy. I'd rather not have anyone poking around, bothering her. You've hired security?"

Well, Dad. "It's taken care of," I said. "Trust me."

She didn't comment on that, but the arch of her narrow eyebrow told me volumes. And I almost shot back with a snarky tell-all where she could shove her attitude. Mom to the rescue once more.

"You don't have to worry about a thing, Vivian," she said, so reassuring the blonde nodded again. "With most of the guests being attached to the show, we have very few outside customers to interfere."

"It's not customers I'm worried about." Was that genuine concern? Did I need to actually take her attitude seriously? "Grace's ex-husband owns a modeling agency and decided to join us at the last minute. They don't exactly have a positive relationship." Ack. Lovely. "He's staying at the lodge, but I'd prefer she didn't have to interact with him. At all." Vivian's cheeks pinked, though she seemed angry, not embarrassed. "I'm positive he's just coming to cause trouble. Grace deserves peace and quiet while she's not working."

"Fair enough," I said. "Consider it done." I'd had my own ex issues in the past and whether the woman was a nightmare guest or a dream, her time at the annex would be my priority.

Vivian seemed reassured, even relented enough to smile at me, before turning to go. Mom left us at the exact moment, giggling with Daisy, while impulse drove me to follow the Queen of Wheat. I caught her elbow, just the barest touch, and she stopped, looking shocked at my audacity, I suppose, while I cleared my throat and spoke in a low voice.

"I'd like to talk to you," I said. "I have questions." Hadn't I just asked myself if my poking around the Pattersons was costing me friendships?

Vivian's expression flattened. "I have to go, Fee."

"You know what I want to talk about." Of course, she did. She'd all but acknowledged her connection the night of the debate when Geoffrey Jenkins backed out of the pending election against Olivia. We'd all been sure she was out, that he was going to be our new mayor, that Crew would be fired, and Robert would be sheriff. Instead, after a disaster that undermined him and a resurgence of support for Olivia, a single phone call at the podium put an end to his attempted coup.

A phone call I was positive came from Vivian French. She shrugged off my touch like I was an annoying fly that she would like to swat. "I'll be along with Grace in a little while," she said. "Make sure her room is ready." And, with that, she swept out of the gym like she really was the queen.

CHAPTER FOUR

"Thank you so much, everyone." Jill wrapped up the class with a hearty hug for Matt who grinned sheepish delight at the embrace while we all cheered his good humor. "You all did amazingly well, and I'm proud of your efforts to learn how to defend yourselves. Now, if you don't mind, I'm going to take this guy home," she winked at him while giggles broke out, "and tend to his bruises."

Matt seemed suddenly happy he'd said yes to being a punching bag.

I lingered in the gym, helping Jill return the floor mats to the stacks against the walls, hearing the excited, happy chatter of the gathered women dissipate as they left in small groups. I grinned at the deputy while she hefted the final mat onto the pile.

"That was awesome," I said. "We really need to do this regularly."

Jill winced and laughed. "I don't think Matt will go for it."

I laughed with her. "No, I didn't mean self-defense classes. But something." I loved the feeling of community I'd sensed in the room. "Some kind of monthly offering that brings us all out and gets us excited like this. Great job, Jill."

She flushed, but beamed, obviously delighted. "Great idea," she said, turning toward where Matt waited for her by the door, rubbing at his ribs like he'd be suffering later, her tender mercies applied or not. "Thanks, Fee. I had fun." She seemed hesitant suddenly, like she wanted to say more, her face scrunching a bit and I waited her out while she chose between speaking and letting it go. "No matter what happens," she finally blurted, "you're my friend. You've always been my friend." And, with that, leaving me mystified and with growing concern, she hurried off to join her boyfriend. The pair left a moment later, Matt waving while I fumbled my own wave back and wondered what was going on.

I'd be calling her later, make no mistake. And she'd be telling me. Yup.

For now, I had the gym to close up, though how I'd been saddled with that responsibility was lost in the hazy initial agreement I'd made to help organize this day in the first place. Daisy was gone, Mom, too, as I exited the gym and headed for home, handing the keys off to Hemmy Stokes, the school custodian who grumbled his unhappy usual mutter incomprehensible to the naked ear and watched me with his beady eyes as I hurried out.

It was a bit of a walk, but I'd run here this morning on purpose, planned to jog the way back as a chance to get my exercise in. I preferred my lakeside runs with Crew, of course, and our now regular workouts with kettlebells—my favorite since using them saved me from death already—but a solitary trot home wasn't a bad thing.

Except, of course, as I stepped out into the sunlight, blinking into the bright March sky and wishing I'd brought my sunglasses while still mulling over Jill's cryptic and troublesome statement, my gaze settled on a familiar sheriff's truck and the handsome man in the driver's seat. Crew waved, grinning, and all thoughts of hoofing it back to Petunia's on my own two feet vanished (along with thoughts of my friend, if I was to be totally and embarrassingly honest) at the prospect of spending time with the man I loved.

Swoon. He really was delicious with his dark hair growing out from the short cut he'd been keeping lately, the length of it sweeping over his collar in that enticing way that begged me to run my fingers through it. His gorgeous blue eyes were hidden behind aviators, the mirrored reflection catching my grin as I leaned into the open window of his cab and kissed him with lingering promise.

Crew kissed me happily back before nuzzling the tip of his nose against my cheek, lips on my ear. "So, think you can kick my ass now, Fleming?"

I laughed, shivering at the soft touch of breath on my skin. "Subdue, at the very least," I said.

He snorted softly, sexy smile tugging at his full lips, the shadow of scruff giving his broad jaw that kind of dark edge that reminded me how delightful it felt to have him kiss me. "I'm all for testing that out."

Growl. And *meow*.

"Need a ride?" He fired up the engine as I circled the front and climbed into the passenger's seat, buckling in after another quick, stolen kiss that only made things worse. Face aching slightly from smiling so much, feeling my heart speed up at the focus I gave his big hand on the steering wheel and the way his broad shoulders tugged at the seams of his shirt, I don't think I could have been any more wrapped up in loving someone as I was Crew Turner.

Just yum.

"Free for dinner tonight?" He drove with expert confidence, one hand on the wheel, the other reaching over to take mine. I loved the warmth of his skin, the faint roughness of callouses on his palm and the softness of the inside of his wrist where his pulse sped up against my fingertips as I settled both hands around his big one.

"Absolutely." We'd been spending a lot of time together since November, an endless string of nights on the sofa in my apartment or at his house, dinners he prepared for me with his capable hands, while not necessarily five-star dining still exactly what I wanted because they were made with love. It felt like we'd gone from sort of dating and wanting to be together to a full-out couple and I couldn't have been happier with how things were going between us. The fact he seemed so eager to pursue our relationship, actively including me in his life, just added to the delightful evolution of us together.

For the first time I knew I'd found exactly who I was meant to spend my life with. And, from the way Crew reciprocated my feelings, he felt the same way.

I hated to leave him as he dropped me off, spending a long, delicious moment enjoying his lips and his hand pressed to the back of my neck, holding me against him while I embraced the tingling delight of endorphins and hormones taking me over and drifted in the joy that was the delicious man kissing me.

When we parted we were both a bit breathless. Okay, I was really breathless and rather giggly. Crew grinned, slipping off his sunglasses to meet my eyes with his brilliant blues. "I love you," he whispered. "Fiona Fleming, I love you so much."

Gasp, choke, inhale. "I love you, too." Take a hike, tears. I kissed him again, softer this time. "I'll see you tonight."

"I'll be waiting." He replaced his glasses and sat back, and it was the hardest thing I'd ever done in my entire life to unbuckle my seatbelt, open the door and slip out onto the sidewalk, to close the door and wave and stand there, watching as he waved back and drove away.

Floating on a cloud of the faint, lingering scent of him and the memory of his lips on mine, I bounded up the steps into Petunia's.

A quick shower and change followed by some of Mom's delicious soup for lunch and I was ready for the influx of guests, namely Vivian's designer friend. Even her uptight warning wasn't enough to diffuse the lasting effect Crew's kisses had on me and when the front door opened, and the foyer flooded with people.

Daisy joined me instantly, her pretty flowered dress her signature, gorgeous dark blonde curls cascading around her. I let her charismatic charm take the lead, staying behind the counter and doing the computer work while she guided the staff to efficiently shift guests from the entry to their rooms. I'd never seen so many stunning young men and women all in one place before, though the lot of them really needed a hamburger, some of them so thin I winced.

As the last of them vanished into the depths of the backyard on their way to the annex, Daisy sighed. "And that's just the assistants and some of the staff," she said, shaking her head, obviously thinking the same thing I was and voicing it like we'd had this conversation going already. Besties. Gotta love them. "It's a hard industry, Fee. I don't envy them. Imagine your whole life hinging on how you look and your age?"

Ack, no thanks. I didn't get to comment as much, though, not when the door opened one last time and

Vivian entered, a tall, slender woman following close behind her.

I was prepared for the worst, naturally. While not exactly rude, the other guests hadn't really been friendly. Which meant Vivian's designer friend was going to be a pain-in-my-rear diva, right? I forced a smile on my face as the Queen of Wheat stepped aside and Grace Fiore fixed me with a beaming smile so open and kind I almost stuttered.

"Ms. Fleming." She hurried toward me, hands outstretched, and captured mine between hers, tugging me closer. I wasn't short by any means at 5'7", but Grace's near six feet coupled with the high heels she wore made me feel positively squat. Not to mention the fact the woman was as slender as a pole, her thin hands strong despite her petite frame. She reminded me of Willow's surprising strength inside such a delicately packaged person, though Grace's impressive height made her seem ethereal and exotic. With full lips glossed with pale pink lipstick and cheekbones that arched under her light green eyes, her tightly bound black hair reminded me of a ballerina preparing for a show. "How delightful to meet you at last. I'm so grateful for your hospitality. And such a lovely residence you have here." Her voice, low and soft, had a faint accent as if she'd spent a lot of time in Europe and picked up the barest trace of foreign influence. "You're so kind to let us take over your business. I always prefer to stay off-venue if possible and you've made my wish come true."

Okay, wow, I hadn't been expecting this at all. While my mind sought out and didn't find a hint of deception, forced to acknowledge nothing about her was disingenuous, I caught my breath and smiled back, knowing I had to be a bit wide-eyed from shock and fighting to recover my professionalism. While wondering if she thought I was fangirling. Which, honestly, I kind of was all of a sudden. Not because she was a famous designer. But because I actually loved her instantly.

"I'm so happy you're here," I said, knowing that came out weird and likely awkward but hoped it might be endearing.

She laughed and hugged me, letting me go finally, though one hand lingered, holding mine like we were old friends while she smiled at Vivian. "This is perfect, Viv," she murmured, squeezing my fingers. "Just perfect. Thank you, darling. You always come through for me." She pressed her lips to Vivian's cheek as the Queen of Wheat smiled back, flushing faintly.

"Anything I can do, Grace," she said. In a tone of voice that made me start. Because she sounded young and sweet and nice and seriously. Like a real person. "Anything at all. You know that." Vivian caught my gaze and flinched ever so faintly as if recognizing I was seeing her soft underbelly at last. "Fiona will take excellent care of you." Ah, there was the commanding tone again. Nice to know she hadn't completely lost her edge.

Grace didn't seem to notice, still holding my

hand. "I'm so jealous," she said, looking back and forth between the two of us with a smile so sweet and lovely I couldn't keep from smiling back. "I wish I lived here, too. How amazing you two awesome women get to spend all this time together." She sighed softly, free hand hooking through Vivian's arm and pulling her close so the three of us stood like we were sisters. "I need more of what you two have in my life."

Um. What had Vivian been telling her about me? From the way the blonde refused to meet my gaze, either she hadn't been telling Grace everything or the designer was jumping to conclusions and Vivian didn't have the heart to tell her otherwise.

Someone cleared their throat and I looked past Grace's slim shoulder toward the young woman waiting behind her. Thick, black rims framed her angular face, dark brown eyes watching from behind the lenses. Her blunt, black bob and abrupt but perfect bangs felt about as haute couture as could be, as did her asymmetrical dress and huge jewelry. She clutched a tablet to her thin chest which she glanced down at when Grace turned to face her.

"Yes, Libby." She seemed amused by the young woman's serious attitude, indulgent as she released Vivian and touched the girl's cheek like she was a small child instead of obviously her assistant.

Libby rolled her eyes. "I take it we have a room to go to?"

Vivian's scowl was instant though Grace laughed and let me go at last to hug Libby who sighed but hugged her back.

"Allow me." Daisy grinned at me while, still in a bit of a daze, I nodded and stepped away. "You're in the annex, Ms. Fiore, Ms. Kim."

"Grace, darling, please." She seemed to notice Daisy for the first time, eyebrows shooting into her hair. "My goodness, you're stunning, my dear."

Was that a flash of jealousy on Vivian's face? Meanwhile, my best friend flushed and giggled.

"Thank you." She gestured for the kitchen door. "Right this way."

Grace paused to lean in and kiss my cheek, her lips cool and soft. "Let's find time for a drink," she said. "I so need strong women in my life." And, with that, she followed Daisy, her assistant trailing after her, Libby's dark gaze scanning me like she was taking my measure before disappearing with her boss through the swinging door.

Leaving me alone with Vivian. Who caught my eyes, her own open and honest for the first time ever, showing me her aching longing for something I couldn't understand. And then, just like that, she shut down, backing away, jaw tightening before she nodded in a sharp up down of her chin.

"Make sure Grace has everything she needs." With that, Vivian spun and left, while I stared after her with more questions than ever before.

CHAPTER FIVE

I drifted into the kitchen and found Daisy returning, joining her and Mom at the counter while my mother worked on a list of needs for the catering job she'd hooked me into.

"I'm so glad you volunteered," Mom said before I could change my mind and tell her she was on her own after all. Not that I would. Maybe if Grace had turned out to be a jerk. But I found myself warming up to the task while Daisy leaned in to look at Mom's list. "Maybe this will finally put an end to the silly animosity between you and Vivian."

Grunt. Though, the visceral reaction I had to Mom's words had no real weight. She was right. Vivian and I were grown women, for goodness's sake. It wasn't like she'd done anything to me that warranted the kind of lingering dislike I'd carried with me my whole life. Even in school, after our initial fight that led to her nose being broken, Vivian had avoided me rather than any actual out-and-out bullying. If I was going to be completely honest, I was being childish about the whole thing.

Blah. Accepting I was a grownup sucked.

Daisy's little grin had a wicked edge. "I think Fee disagrees."

Mom tsked at me, her frown enough disappointed teacher I relented. "You need to let go of the past, Fiona," she said. "You're missing out on a great opportunity, both of you." She patted my hand, nodded to Daisy. "All three of you. Vivian isn't the devil, girls. She's a powerful, driven, wonderful woman doing her very best, just like we are. She's had no support in this town, had to do everything herself. If anything, she's met with more resistance than we could ever imagine." I didn't know that and had a guilty moment of recalling Crew's troubles with the town comparing him to Dad, how a lot of things went on behind the scenes I had no idea about. Had Vivian faced the same kind of conflict when she'd taken over her family's business? "If you just took a moment and saw things from her perspective, I think you'd actually like her, Fee."

Eep. Mom was right and yet. The Patterson question loomed. Instead of arguing, I turned with gratitude at the sound of the bell as someone arrived in the foyer. I hurried to my new guest, mulling over Mom's words while smiling my professional best at yet another thin, tall woman here to take over my B&B. Except, instead of looking calm and confident, this one seemed nervous, or at least secretive as she slipped her huge sunglasses free from her eyes, faint dark circles under the pale blue of her slightly sunken gaze. Her cheekbones stood out so prominently I wondered when she'd eaten a solid meal last, her dark hair tucked under a scarf.

"Noel Lewder," she said, voice breathy and slightly nasal. "I have a reservation."

"Nice to meet you." I offered my hand which she hesitated to shake, her grip almost non-existent when she did a quick up and down before jerking her fingers from mine. "Fiona Fleming, your host. I have you booked in upstairs here at Petunia's. Can we help with your bag?"

Noel shook her head, a lock of glossy hair falling free of her scarf. She might have been bone thin, but she really was beautiful, in a waif-like, vulnerable way, her pale skin flawless, lips so full they seemed to dominate the lower half of her face. "I'm fine, thank you."

"The other models are staying at the lodge," I said. "Are you sure you'd rather be here? We can arrange it if you'd like to be closer to the show."

The flash of rage that crossed her face actually took me aback, one hand pressing to my heart. Noel recovered visibly from her reaction, but her voice was cold when she answered.

"I'm not a model," she snapped, taking her key from my hand and turning toward the stairs. "And

I'll ask you to mind your own business."

Wow. So, I'd been expecting divas, and looked like I'd finally found one. Though her insistence she wasn't a model was clearly a lie. Or maybe she was a wannabe? Maybe she had been one and wasn't anymore? Whatever. I let her go, shrugging off her reaction, hearing the painful thud of her suitcase up the steps and wishing I could just carry the damned thing for her so she wouldn't hit every single stair so thoroughly.

Well, I couldn't expect everyone to be like Grace, I suppose. And if Noel was the only mean girl in the lot, I'd take it. I finished logging her into the computer as the door swept open one more time. I plastered on another smile, ready to face down whatever came my way and stopped, startled, staring, smile forgotten, at the sight of the familiar young woman standing in my foyer.

Mila Martin smiled back at me, huge eyes wide and glossy behind the shine of her glasses, acne still in full blossom on her round cheeks, the brown cardigan, calf-length skirt and comfortable looking shoes doing little to improve her appearance. Neither did the thin, brown ponytail she wore. But wait a second, hadn't I just chastised myself for being shallow about appearances with Alice Moore? And here I was doing the same for the young woman in my foyer. I hadn't seen her in two years, not since the death of Skip Anderson. She'd been stalking Willow Pink at the time, one of those super fans who had crossed over the line from adoration to creepiness and from what I'd heard she'd run into issues with the law because of her behavior. She was the last person I'd expected to find at Petunia's, and I had a flash of curiosity and then concern that maybe she'd attached to someone new.

Please, don't let it be Grace. Vivian would lose her mind.

"Fee." Mila hurried toward me in lurching delight, hugging me like we were old friends. I hugged her back, feeling her trembling when I released her and took in the dark circles under her big eyes, the thinness of her body. She hadn't been a big woman to begin with, but she seemed to have shrunk, gaze burning with an internal fire that kept her going when maybe she should have been somewhere she could lie down for a while.

"Mila." I tried a smile and felt the million watts of her returning grin hit me like a blow.

"You remember me!" She tried to hug me again, but I dodged, fending her off and putting the computer counter between us. Mila didn't seem to notice, her stare locked on my face. "I'm so happy to see you again, Fee."

"How have you been?" This was super weird, and the creep factor was growing by the moment.

Mila shrugged off the question, eyes never leaving my face. "I was in an institution for a while," she said like she was telling me the weather outside. "Court ordered."

"I see." What to say to that? "Because of Willow?" Nice, Fee. Way to be an insensitive jerk.

But Mila just smiled wider. "Oh, her," she said, like her stalking addiction toward the star had no lingering effect. Well, that was good, right? Was she cured? "I'm so over *her*. I've moved on."

Nice to hear. Wait, did that mean she'd latched onto someone else for real? My heart beat a bit faster as I thought about Grace. Could I keep Mila away from her?

"I have a reservation." She batted her lashes at me. "Here at Petunia's. I made sure to pick Petunia's, not the annex. It's under Marion. That's my real name."

I checked the listing and secretly hoped it wouldn't be there. Nope, no such luck. "All set," I said, a bit too cheerfully but Mila just seemed delighted. Subtle social cues were not her strong suit, apparently. I handed her a key and when she took it from me her fingers lingered.

"I'm so happy to be back in Reading." She stared, a full-on stare like she'd gotten lost in a drug haze, or someone hit her in the head. Was she on meds? Yikes, I had to keep an eye on her, just in case. "So happy, Fee."

I nodded, waited for her to leave. To take her bag and go upstairs to her room. While she stood there and smiled at me in a dreamy way that just got weirder and more awkward by the second.

I finally cleared my throat and gestured for the stairs. "Have a nice stay."

"Thank you." She left then, though she didn't stop staring as she headed for the steps, dragging her bag behind her, and continued to watch me as she ascended to the second floor. I shivered a bit at the intensity of her gaze, thoroughly creeped out.

I finally shrugged off the effect of her odd behavior. You know what? I wasn't responsible for Mila. If she was here for Grace, then Grace would have to deal with her. Not my problem. But I would be warning Dad, just in case. He'd agreed to keep an eye on things, though the need for actual security had seemed excessive to me.

Whatever. I had more important things to consider as I checked my watch and grinned to myself before heading for the door to my apartment. I had a date, after all, and there was no better way to distract myself from the world around me than spending time with the man I loved.

CHAPTER SIX

I settled into my seat, smiling at the hostess who set a menu in front of me before doing the same for Crew. "Your server will be right with you." She left us alone then, the soft music and low lighting of the rooftop restaurant about as romantic as any setting I could have imagined.

When Crew texted me while I tried to decide what to wear to dinner, I'd been surprised by his suggestion we eat out. He usually liked to cook for me, though we had gone out a few times. I never knew if it was concern that Reading residents might see us together—old fears—or if he just wanted me all to himself—I preferred that reasoning—but whatever the case, we always seemed to end up on his couch or mine.

My initial disappointment had turned to delight at the suggestion we try out Rooftop, Alicia's latest project. The glassed-in space at the top of the lodge had a spectacular view of the mountains, Cutter Lake in the distance, the last of the snow from the most recent storm shining under the moon and stars. Late March or not, the weather had been spectacular, warmer than usual, and the skiing hill wasn't as active as usual despite efforts to make snow to keep visitors happy. I was delighted, because it meant we were able to get reservations, even with the extra guests the fashion show event had brought in.

Crew seemed oddly uncomfortable in his dark suit despite the fact I knew he'd spent many years wearing one while working with the FBI. He'd asked me what color I was wearing and surprised me by matching his pocket square and tie to the navy blue of my dress. A sweet detail, one that made my heart melt as much as this effort to make our date special.

Moments later, drinks ordered, he saluted me with his wine glass, blue eyes intent. He'd taken the seat next to me, rather than across from me at the small table near the bubbling fountain at the far side of the restaurant, his chair tucked close to mine while he leaned in, the scent of his cologne as swoon-worthy as it was subtle. The man was just hot, there were no two ways about it, and I found myself staring at his lips and wishing we'd eaten at home after all.

"You look beautiful." He cleared his throat, smiled, looked away. "Fee, there's something I wanted to talk to you about." Crew coughed softly again, so adorable in his discomfort I reached out and took his hand.

"Whatever it is," I said, "we'll be okay." My mind, meanwhile, spun out some unhappy scenarios which I then firmly smothered in my love for him. I was done doubting us, had given that up in November when I'd finally shed the influence of my ex, Ryan Richards. I loved Crew. And I meant what I said. "We'll always be okay."

Crew's face softened, his smile sweet, almost young, like he'd just let go of something himself. "There's nothing wrong," he said. "Everything is right." Crew hesitated, sat back, then forward again, like he struggled to get comfortable in his own skin suddenly. His hand tightened around mine and he laughed then, boyish grin making his eyes sparkle. "I love you."

"I love you, too." Weird. But then again, my day had been like that, so I'd take it.

We were interrupted by our server, a perky girl who was, at the same time, efficient. Crew's odd mood seemed to have passed and we spent the next hour or so laughing, sampling each other's dinners and talking about the kinds of nothings that made me feel closer to him than ever.

The only downside to our date was the occasional interruption in the form of other guests at the lodge. Namely, of the model variety. It was easy to pick them out in their perfect clothes and uber skinny bodies with their just a bit too loud voices and gathered packs of society's ideal for beauty collected at tables like clusters of peacocks looking for adoration. Crew's occasional glance their way had nothing to do with attraction and everything, it seemed, with irritation. Nice to know the man I loved was that into me, right?

I did welcome one short moment of intrusion, though, when Grace spotted us and came to the table, Crew didn't seem as willing to share me as I was to share him. But he was gracious when I introduced him to the designer and her kind expression seemed to ease his cool welcome.

"How darling you two are together." She loved that word, apparently. "Just gorgeous, Fee. And so much love for each other, it's as clear as the smiles on your faces." She sighed then and clasped her hands in front of her chest, huge eyes flickering back and forth between us. "Jealous again, my dear." She offered me a cheek kiss.

I couldn't help the giggle that escaped. "He'll do." I offered Crew an arched eyebrow and a wink and he grinned back.

"I guess," he said, laughing. "In a pinch."

Grace hugged me around the shoulders with one arm like we'd known each other forever and I didn't resist because, oddly, it felt true. "Delicious," she said, a wicked edge to her voice. "I see a great future ahead for you two."

"Only if Fee can stay out of trouble," Crew growled in that gravel voice of his.

Grace gasped softly, eyes wide. "Yes, Vivian told

me all about your penchant for dead bodies and putting your life at risk, my darling Fiona. You really must be more careful, promise me."

I shrugged. "Doing my best," I said. "I think I'm just cursed or something."

Grace pinched my cheek ever so softly before letting me go. "Nonsense," she said. "Remarkable, brilliant, stunning. I don't believe in curses."

Okay, totally in love with her, thanks.

Before I could come up with a witty reply, however, Grace's attention was caught by someone entering the restaurant and I instantly felt protective of her as she shivered just a little and sagged somewhat, though it only lasted a moment. Her beautiful face settled into contented confidence while I followed her gaze to the entry and the tall, silver-haired man who'd just walked in, a model on either arm. Statuesque, handsome in his dark suit, he obviously had some emotional meaning for her.

And then it clicked. Her ex-husband. Had to be. I recognized her physical reaction on a purely emotional level. A moment later his eyes met hers and I had my confirmation.

"Hang onto love, Fee," she whispered to me as she let me go. "It's more precious than you know and when it's gone, it's gone forever." She left me then, nodding to Crew before crossing the rooftop to greet the newcomer. It was obvious he wasn't happy to see Grace, though they were too far away to catch what they were saying to each other. Crew seemed unhappy, restless, and when Grace's ex reached out to touch her, the sheriff half stood up. Yeah, it looked bad all the way over hear, Crew's protective instincts clearly stirred.

But before he could interfere, the familiar sight of Matt and Jill appeared, flanking the tall, silver-haired agent. Instead of their usual uniforms—park ranger and deputy respectively—they were both in suits, more like federal agents than local law enforcement. And I realized as they got between the pair they were on duty, though from the look on Crew's face he hadn't known Jill was moonlighting as security.

And wasn't all that happy to find out this way. Since when were they at odds? I was reminded of her weird comment this morning and had to wonder if the two were connected. Had to be. What did her moonlighting have to do with being my friend?

"You okay?" I reached out, took his hand again but he shrugged off my question, tone a bit sharp as he replied.

"Fine," he said. "I don't want to talk about it. Not tonight." His smile was quick, apologetic. "Not tonight."

Okay then. "Do you know anything about Grace's ex?" Yeah, bring up work, Fee.

Crew didn't seem to mind that question. "Name's Henry Ostler," he said with a wry grin. "You better believe Vivian stopped by my office with a dossier she'd assembled herself on everyone here who might be a threat to her friend." Of course, she had. "I should hire her. She's way better at presenting evidence than my deputies." Whoa, that was a shot at

Robert, yes, but at Jill, too? What was up? And why hadn't he said he was having problems with her?

I wanted to ask that very question, his request we keep it out of our conversation tonight or not, when a stir at the door caught my attention for the second time. This entrance was met with chatter from the models and more disruption that Jill and Matt seemed to find almost more than they could handle. Again, whatever was being said was indecipherable, but it was pretty clear from the anger in Grace's carriage, from the stiff and threatening posture her ex-husband wore and how the newcomer—another older man with wavy white hair longer than typical in a bright blue suit and tie that could have lit up the mountain—faced off with both of them there was old, bad blood on the verge of being spilled any second now.

Crew's jaw jumped when I turned back to him. "Frederick Newmark," he said, though he didn't seem happy anymore to talk about the pending drama. "Old designer, repped by Henry and a rival to Grace. And now I'm apparently living and working in a soap opera. Awesome."

I laughed to try to ease the mood. "What else is new?"

My boyfriend hesitated before snorting and nodding with a grin returning. "Right," he said. "Just another day at the office."

"Absolutely," I said, leaning in to kiss his cheek. "It wouldn't be us if there wasn't drama."

Crew's blue eyes, instead of smiling back,

suddenly darkened, his pupils growing in a flash of emotion I couldn't read. The intensity of his stare made me freeze, heart thudding painfully as I tried to breathe, couldn't, waiting for him to let me go from the grasp of his blue eyes.

He opened his mouth, parted those luscious lips, inhaled as if to speak. I hung on the instant, all at once excited and terrified of what he might say. Knowing whatever it was, no matter what, I loved him with all my heart. Even if what he had to say was going to leave me in tears, happy or otherwise.

CHAPTER SEVEN

Crew didn't get to tell me what he wanted to. Instead, I was left hanging as Alicia and Jared appeared at our table as if by magic. Clearly, I'd been so wrapped up in my boyfriend I'd failed to see the two approach. I stood and hugged them when I got over my disappointment they'd intruded on what was clearly an important moment. Crew wasn't so gracious, at least not at first, though he did join me and shake Jared's hand when I let the tall, handsome contractor go.

"So sorry," Alicia said almost instantly as if registering she'd broken up a moment between me and Crew. "We wanted to check and see how dinner was, if you're having fun." She flinched slightly at the raised voices by the door while Jared frowned in that direction. I didn't often see him in a suit, either, though Alicia was often in one. The slim, knee-length satin number she wore tonight made her look tiny compared to her fiancé. What was it about a suit that made a man so freaking yummy? "And to apologize for the disturbance."

I shook my head, smiling to reassure her, feeling the distance that had grown between the three of us vanish as Alicia caught my hand and smiled back. I was imagining things, obviously. They just felt bad for backing out of using the annex, something I could care less about as long as they were happy.

"We love it up here, Alicia," I said, hoping I gushed enough. She beamed, so I did my job, Jared smiling down at her with that kind of indulgent sweetness that made them adorable together. "Don't we, Crew?"

He mumbled something while Alicia eye-rolled and laughed.

"Thank you," she said, words tumbling out while she punctuated her excited talk with giggles. "It's been a labor of love, but I couldn't wait to open up and see what people thought. It's going to be stunning this summer when we retract the roof."

I glanced up at the greenhouse-like panels and realized only then it had that capability. Wow, talk about expensive. At least, I was guessing. But neither seemed concerned by the cost so they had to be doing well. Good for them. They weren't the only ones.

Smug much, Fiona Fleming?

And yet, they'd lost their chef and Alicia was suffering from some kind of inferiority complex when it came to Vivian French. This town made my head hurt.

"You must be thrilled to have the fashion show preview here at the lodge?" I gestured for them to join us, but Jared shook his head, Alicia sighing through pursed lips.

"Honestly, I'm just over it all, Fee," she said, voice down. "I've never had so many problems with guests in my entire life." Because she was ancient and jaded and all that. Well, come to think of it she'd been running the lodge for two summers. That gave her permission to play old hat. "Truth be told, I wanted to be a model when I was little. I used to fangirl over Vivian, you know. But I'm happy being a businesswoman. Right, sweetie?"

Jared hugged her. "I wouldn't want to share you with the world like that," he said. "You're all mine."

She giggled again while my mind tripped around her comment about the Queen of Wheat as I thought about her snide comment to Alicia that very morning. If Alicia was a fan, why did Vivian treat her so coldly? Maybe I'd been without a murder to solve for too long. Never mind the pending mysteries I'd let sit on the back burner. Something about a fresh conundrum always got me going for some reason.

"What did you mean, fangirling over Vivian?" What was I missing?

Alicia was clearly surprised by my question. "She was a model years ago. You didn't know?"

Um, nope. Vivian, a model, really? I mean, sure, she was beautiful and everything. But I had no idea. I'd lost track of the cheer girl when I'd left home after high school. And it wasn't like we'd been friends or kept up with each other or anything. I hadn't seen Vivian in years and only reconnected with her—if you wanted to call it that—when I moved home to Reading.

"Well, she was a rising star," Alicia said, clearly excited to fill me in on the details while Jared made a face at Crew who made one right back. Boys. My friend ignored them and went on, one hand on my forearm. "From what I heard she was on track to be one of the top runway models."

"What happened?" I glanced at the disaster still going on at the entry. Jill and Matt seemed to have the mess in hand, but the three hadn't parted ways and the conversation continued, heated if quieter.

"I'm not sure," she said. "Oh, do you know Mateo Marney?" She sighed as she pointed out a handsome Latino man who laughed as he ate, surrounded by models who didn't. Eat, that was. Or laugh. Poor things. "He's an up-and-comer, one of Henry's newest talents. I wonder why Kami Derham is eating with him." She sniffed. "She's a favorite of Grace's. That's loyalty for you."

Jared chuckled, index finger booping her nose. "I thought you said you were over the whole thing?" He was clearly teasing her and yet I agreed with him. For someone who didn't care about the modeling world she seemed to be firmly planted in the know.

Alicia shrugged, winked at me. "A girl has to stay on top of her game. It's my job to know my clients, right?"

If she said so. I was happy to just give mine a roof in exchange for their money, thanks. They could keep their drama to themselves.

"Ooh, this will be good." Another tall, skinny young woman, this one blonde in comparison, stalked toward Mateo, leaning in to say something clearly angry to the girl Alicia identified as Kami. Kami, in turn, her dark hair piled around her in a frothing wave of curls, said something back that visibly upset the intruder. "That's Faith Leeman. She's supposed to be Mateo's girlfriend as well as his body model for all his work."

They looked pretty identical to me despite their difference in hair color. Both gorgeous, both young, both too skinny for their own good. Kami stood up and tossed down her napkin to the table, though it was clear she hadn't eaten a bite of the food on her plate, and stormed off, pushing past Grace who only then noticed she was there. But I wasn't interested in Kami's departure when I spoke again.

"Any idea what happened between Grace and Henry?" She'd seemed so sad when she'd talked to me about love. Did she still have feelings for her ex? He was handsome, I'd give him that, but the cold expression on his face reminded me of a statue, not a loving partner.

Man, I was so lucky, wasn't I?

"I hear she dumped him because he disagreed

with the way her designs were going." Alicia bit her lower lip, the two of us watching the drama unfold while I wished for subtitles. "So sad. I heard they were desperately in love with each other once upon a time."

Very sad. I glanced at Crew and caught his dark expression, his frustration, and snapped myself out of the unfolding story across the room, reaching out to take his hand. Better to focus on my own tale to tell, thanks. He met my eyes, his softening, though he was still irritable enough he didn't smile.

The volume escalated all over again as Grace turned toward Henry. This time I caught the words, "*My* fault?" Alicia flinched and grasped for Jared's arm while poor Jill and Matt looked frustrated about what they could even do.

"Excuse us," Alicia said, saying, "enjoy the rest of your dinner!" over one shoulder as she and Jared hurried to the knot of unhappiness.

For a single instant, I longed to go with them, to find out what was happening. Until I took firm hold of myself and spun, back to the whole silly thing and cupped Crew's face in my hands. He looked down at me, shoulders stiff, but didn't resist when I kissed him. He softened against me, sinking down into his chair when I let him go and purposely took the other seat, the one that ensured I was facing him and the mountain and couldn't see a thing happening at the entry. Because he deserved my full attention, and he was all I cared about.

Yup. I picked love over being a busybody. Go

figure.

Crew glanced at the fight then back at me before a slow, sexy smile crossed his lips. "Got it," he whispered.

"You betcha," I said, surprised to find I was a bit choked up, to be honest. He had to know I put him first. Had to. Because there was no way he'd ever have to wonder if I loved him more than poking my nose into other people's business. No contest. Not now, and not ever.

Whatever Crew had planned to talk to me about didn't come up, though we did manage to enjoy the rest of our dinner and our shared slice of chocolate cheesecake, the unfolding drama long over by the time we finished and rose to go.

It was a quiet ride home and I hoped he'd say yes when I invited him in, but Crew shook his head instead, not meeting my eyes, head down.

"Can't tonight," he said, voice rough enough I knew something was wrong. I really needed to insist he tell me, but when he looked up and met my gaze, his was soft, sweet, loving, so I let him have his retreat and, after a lovely kiss missing the usual heat I felt for him, if none of the adoring connection, I found myself again on the sidewalk, waving as Crew drove away.

CHAPTER EIGHT

My phone rang when I stepped into the foyer of Petunia's but when I tried to answer, the caller cut off. I checked the number, only to find it listed as unknown. Weird, but then again, random wrong numbers happened all the time, so it wasn't a big deal.

I did a quick walkthrough of the main building before slipping outside with Petunia into the cold night air and crossing to the annex. The young woman on the desk for the evening nodded pleasantly to me, but I didn't stop to talk to Briana, instead returning to Petunia's satisfied all was well in the world. At least, in my business.

I'd come a long way in trusting and in believing in my relationship with Crew, in shedding Ryan's influence and the hurt he'd inflicted, but it was hard not to let doubt creep in after the odd and uncomfortable ending to my night with the man I loved so much it hurt. I hesitated to text him, finally sent a heart emoji. Seconds later he texted back.

Talk tomorrow? And then, a moment later: *You were so beautiful tonight, Fee. Breathlessly.*

Gulp and gosh golly gee shucks, shiver. *You need to wear a suit more often.*

I sank to the bed, Petunia panting her way up the steps to sit beside me, as Crew responded.

Tried that, he sent. *Prefer the khaki. Keeps me closer to the woman I love.*

In other words, Reading over the FBI? Oh, Crew.

Good night, beautiful, he sent. *Love you.*

As if there was any doubt whatsoever. Get a grip, Fleming. *Good night, handsome. Love you, too.*

And, with that, all was right in my world after all.

The next morning, car loaded with supplies, I drove while Mom chattered at my side, our short jaunt to the lodge just long enough for her to fill me in on her cooking plans while I could barely fit in nods and grunts of agreement. At least it seemed Alicia had given her permission to use the kitchen at the lodge, so maybe my young friend knew losing Carol as her chef wasn't in her best interest. None of my business, but I still wondered, though Mom didn't mention anything further as she snapped orders at the two kitchen workers who helped carry her goodies in the back doors.

It was pretty clear from the disarray in the kitchen the loss of their chef was making things difficult. I didn't recognize the man who seemed to have taken over and though the food I'd eaten last night was delicious, if he was the new chef, his organizational skills left a lot to be desired. I could see a head-butting session forming between him and Mom almost immediately.

"I've been told I have a space to work in." Mom started out nice enough. The tall, skinny man with the mustache and arrogant attitude wasn't having any.

"This is *my* kitchen," he snapped. "Who are you, exactly?"

"Lucy Fleming." She tried for firm, hand extended. He had no idea the olive branch she was offering. Instead, he sniffed at her like she offended him just by being there and turned his back.

"Chef Paul Entrant," he said like we should know who he was and if we didn't, we were utter Luddites who didn't deserve to breathe his air. "And now, you will leave my kitchen and not return."

I could have argued. I could have snapped and fought and snarled. Instead, I went in search of Alicia.

Yes, I left my mother to fend for herself. Thing was, I didn't need the lodge's manager to save Mom. If she valued the chef she had, Alicia would come to the kitchen right now and keep my mother from murdering Chef Paul before his untimely demise put a kink in Mom's prep time.

I'd had enough dead bodies on my hands the last few years, thanks. Besides, arrogant asshats deserved to be pulled down a few pegs by those who employed them. This was Alicia's job, not mine. Crew would be proud of me, wouldn't he? I know I was pretty freaking smugly proud of myself, thank you very much. So much, in fact, I almost missed the hissing argument going on between three familiar women at the end of the service corridor outside the kitchen door.

I knew this corridor well, had found myself pushed out the doors at the far end and into a snowstorm two Valentine's Days ago, almost dying of exposure in the process. This time, though, it wasn't a physical threat I faced, but the dagger stares of the three who I'd either met or had been pointed out to me the night before. Kami and Faith seemed about the same, though much less put together than at dinner. But their matching skinny bodies and almost identical casual yoga pants and tanks under overlarge sweater outfits could have been a uniform. As for Libby, Grace's assistant, she was too far on the Goth side this morning to look like she fit in. Wait, why were they conversing if Faith worked for Mateo? Was she switching sides? Before I could ponder further or even walk past and out of the drama altogether, the tall, handsome form of Henry Ostler brushed past me and joined them.

Oh, really? Libby's eyes met mine as I arched one brow at her. So, she was talking to Grace's ex behind her boss's back? Classy. Libby looked away, Faith and Kami both ignoring me before going their separate ways while Henry bent his head and began to whisper to Libby.

I could have poked my nose in, wanted to more than anything. And, instead, walked away in search of Alicia. Because the new and improved and in love Fiona Fleming minded her own business when it wasn't required otherwise. Let them conspire and do their little betrayal dance. You betcha I'd be warning Grace about her assistant, though. At least mentioning her clandestine meeting with Henry would put my mind at ease. But that was the extent of my involvement, sure was.

Alicia was easy to find and, after telling her what was going on—probably devolving as we spoke—in her kitchen, the young blonde huffed a furious sigh and stomped her way into the chef's domain. She didn't berate him publically, but when he spluttered his attempt to shut her down, she grasped his arm in a hand of steel—I'd been on the other side of her hand in self-defense class, so I was aware of her strength—and jerked him into the small office at the far end of the room before firmly closing the door. Mom smiled at me, though her face was tight with suppressed anger as the remainder of the staff avoided both of us like we had an illness they didn't want to contract. Five minutes later, after a brief outburst of Alicia shrieking behind the door she emerged like nothing had happened, smile plastered firmly in place, one hand taking Mom's as she patted her other with a professional and apologetic smile.

"He gives you an ounce of trouble," she hissed around her pleasant expression, "and I'm firing his ass. Okies?"

Mom nodded, equally collected. "Thank you, dear," she said. "I'd love to get to work now."

If it was me? I would have just held a grudge and stayed out of his way. My mother didn't operate like that. After about a half-hour cooling-off period in which Chef Paul snapped continually at his people, my mother proceeded to court him in a way that made my jaw ache from trying not to laugh out loud.

"Chef Paul, you're so talented, could you…?"

"Chef Paul, I know you're far more skilled than I, would you…?"

"Chef Paul, I just know you have a wonderful idea…"

Thing was? It worked. Within another half-hour, my mother and the arrogant chef were besties while he softened his attitude, his staff breathed a sigh of relief and my mother—my clever, brilliant and kind-hearted mother—did her best Lucy Fleming and made him her friend.

I was about to suggest she didn't need me anymore when Vivian swept into the kitchen. The chef's instant unhappiness stirred my worry, but Mom's instant happy greeting cooled his jets and sent him off to finish the task she assigned him while making him think it was his idea.

I really had to take Lucy lessons. And hey, wait a second. Did she use these tactics on me…?

Libby followed Vivian in, catching my eyes with a frown on her face. She was probably going to ask me to keep my mouth shut, right? That what I'd seen wasn't what I thought it was? Whatever. I purposely looked away while Vivian spoke to Mom. Let Grace's traitor assistant be uncomfortable. I already loved the designer and refused to let the girl who was supposed to have her back catch even a hint of relief.

"How are we coming with lunch preparations?" Vivian seemed slightly off, almost nervous while Mom patted her hand in reassurance.

"Splendidly," she said. I kept my mouth shut, hoping she wasn't just saying that to make Vivian feel better. "We're on time and will be setting up shortly. I've personally prepared Grace's menu as requested, Vivian. Was there anything else?"

"Grace can't have seafood." Libby stepped forward, frowning. "It makes her ill."

"I'm well aware of that," Vivian snapped, not even looking at her, clearly unhappy with the girl. Huh. Did she know Libby wasn't faithful to her boss, had been talking privately with Henry? Possibly. Well, we were on the same side there, at least. Maybe there was hope for us yet.

"I'm trying to make sure my employer doesn't get sick," Libby shot back.

"And I'm trying to make sure Grace has the kind of support she needs and deserves." Okay then, that would be a yes on the knowing Libby was a traitor thing.

The young assistant grumbled something but instead of fighting with Vivian turned and stomped out, not a scrap of graceful femininity to her despite her heels and elaborate Goth styling I realized was a fashion show of its own.

"Everything all right, dear?" Mom paused to show Vivian compassion, Olivia sweeping past the departing Libby and striding toward us while Chef Paul snarled something about his kitchen turning into a common area.

Vivian almost said something, but Olivia was already interrupting.

"I don't like it, Vivian," the mayor snapped, loud enough everyone heard her like she didn't care if we knew she and the Queen of Wheat were on the outs. "This whole conflict situation means trouble. You said your designer friend would bring attention to Reading. I'm not looking for the sort of negative press her disaster of a love life can mean for us."

Right, because Olivia's little fiasco with Willow and that utterly charming jerk of a husband of hers who'd died in my arms wasn't dramatic negative press that swallowed Reading whole and spit us out the other side.

Vivian didn't argue with the mayor, though, turning to face off with the cream-suited, dark-bobbed older woman, her own fitted two-piece in soft pink making her look like a princess compared to Olivia's polished and practiced politician persona.

"Whatever your concerns," Vivian said, voice as

cold as I'd ever heard it, "I assure you they are baseless. This is an excellent opportunity for Reading, Olivia, and you know it."

"We'll see." Hmmm. There was more to this, wasn't there, than the mayor's worries? And that was when I realized I'd been thick about the whole thing, hadn't I? Olivia trusted Vivian, included her in our little gathering of powerful women back in November when Olivia feared she'd lose her seat as mayor. Only to find out that Vivian wasn't exactly playing for our team. I didn't have confirmation of that, of course. But did Olivia? And, if so, were they now enemies? I'd had my heart buried in Crew Turner the last four months—had I missed their falling out and was only now catching up?

Olivia seemed like she wanted to say more but didn't. Instead, with a huff, she spun and left, Vivian staring after her, while I struggled with my own sense of loyalty toward the woman who kept my B&B rooms full and the pink-clad one my mother assured me I'd misjudged my whole life.

Huh. Wasn't expecting to feel bad for Vivian French. Go figure.

CHAPTER NINE

I stayed firmly out of the way while my curiosity about the behind-the-scenes process of running a fashion show got the better of me, though I had to admit as I lurked and watched the models doing their catwalk best while being berated and sometimes belittled by their handlers, I found myself becoming rapidly disillusioned by the whole thing.

Sure, I'd had kind of the same experience last winter when my mother had been purposely sabotaged by a fellow contestant on *Bake or Break*, the cooking show that ended this season thanks, it was said, to the death of head judge Ron Williams. Even though it came out he was a thief and a fraud, his popularity with the viewing public had obviously been the driving force behind the success of the show, something it couldn't survive.

Somehow, I didn't think this fashion show was going to suffer the same fate. Yes, the designers were the keys to the brands, but it was the continual evolution of *haute couture*, from what I could tell, that was the real star. I felt almost dizzy at the cookie-cutter appearance of the bone-thin young men and women who sported the same flat, empty expression while moving their bodies in unnatural struts like giraffes attempting to walk straight on stilts.

I ran a few snacks for Mom, lugging bottles of water, trying to stay out of the way. When I accidentally tripped over the hanging strap of a designer purse, the owner was quick to tell me what she thought of my attention to detail.

"That's a Richon bag!" Faith Leeman's gorgeous face wasn't looking so pretty as she practically spit her disdain in my direction. She had no idea how close she was to wearing that flat of water bottles on her nasty little head.

"How nice for you," I said, dropping the weight on the table next to her and frowning in return. "I'm sure you're very happy together." Snort.

I'd never seen anyone turn so red before. It was fascinating to watch. "How dare you? I'll have you fired!"

"Oh, please," I said. "Please. Get me fired. *Please.*" That would have been awesome. Hey, wait a minute. I could leave any time I wanted. Nope. Wait. Mom. Sigh.

Faith's painted upper lip turned into a snarl as she

spun with her back to me, her hands fishing around in her poor, clearly badly put-upon bag. "I want your name."

"And I want to go home." I'd had enough of this little game, ready to stride off and leave her behind. But my attempt at a powerful and collected retreat was almost undone as my sneaker struck something slippery and I shrieked while windmilling my arms to keep from falling.

When I finally caught my balance and looked down, Faith's scream of rage emerged louder than my own declaration of surprise. She lunged for my foot and jerked the shiny pink notebook out from under my toes, hugging it to her chest while she glanced around like someone might have seen something they weren't supposed to. When she met my eyes again, she was still furious.

"That's it," she snarled. "I'm calling security."

"Don't bother," I snapped back. "If you think I'm the one that's getting kicked out, you're sadly mistaken." Okay, so I could have tried to be nicer, more accommodating, patient. Could have.

Argh.

Mom took one look at my face when I returned to the kitchen and sighed. "Just take a break, honey," she said, not even wanting to ask me what happened. And you know what? I didn't really want to talk about it anyway. Bad enough I agreed to help and was yet again treated like crap by someone who thought they were better than me. I was actually going to just cut and go home but instead grumbled my way outside for ten minutes to cool off.

When I came back, it was to a boring stint of doing not much while Mom continued her emotional control over the chef and his kitchen. I wandered off and, though I still didn't know why I was being a sucker for punishment, I returned to the ballroom to hide in the corner and watch the models being directed down the catwalk. I was surprised to find Vivian also watching, her own expression empty, though the way her knuckles whitened on the forearms of her tailored jacket where she gripped herself like she was some kind of lifeline, she wasn't enjoying the view. I approached with vague trepidation but more curiosity, thanks to Alicia's information from the night before, and received another surprise when the Queen of Wheat didn't immediately walk away from me.

Instead, Vivian nodded to the line of humanity our society deemed the perfect body type and sighed ever so softly. "They've just gotten skinnier over the years," she said, sounding sad, to be honest. "Yes, we were expected to be thin, but I never felt as though I was unhealthy."

"I had no idea you were in the fashion industry." I was going to say, "I didn't know you modeled," but changed my mind at the last second, hoping my terminology would encourage conversation. Not that I cared what Vivian had done, though, right? Sure, Fee. Not in active busybody mode at the moment or anything.

Vivian shrugged, though her face softened, the

tightness she usually wore dissipating and leaving her about as human as I'd ever seen her. "I was scouted in high school," she said. "By Henry Ostler." Grunt, no way. "It's how I met Grace. She was one of his new designers, and I started out modeling for her."

That filled in a lot of blanks. "Any idea what happened between them?"

Vivian's faint scowl wasn't angry, more sorrowful. "I don't know," she said, "not officially. They were so in love, more than anyone I'd ever met. I suppose when that depth of emotion turns, it does so quickly and without remorse. Whatever the case, they haven't spoken a civil word to each other since she asked for a divorce three years ago."

"How long did you model for her?" Was I really asking out of mere curiosity and not my own need to dig into Vivian's life? I wasn't expecting this much compassion, not for her, despite the softening I'd felt toward her the past year or so. Vivian glanced at me, looking surprised. By my tone? Maybe. But it didn't trigger her retreat as I expected. Instead, she answered like she wasn't planning on leaving me hanging.

"Three years," she said, that longing in her eyes now lurking in her voice, much as we physically lingered in the wings. "Endless fashion shows, from New York to Milan to London and beyond." Wow, I had no idea. None. "It might not look like it, but doing this job takes more talent and discipline than many people think."

I had zero doubt of that. One of the models had

donned a pair of giant shoes that had no heels, only a gap behind her foot with a silver platform beneath her toes. She wobbled a few times but made the circuit without falling, something I was certain I could never do, no matter how much practice I had.

"This is the new age of fashion, Fee," Vivian said, voice vibrating with something that sounded like pride but tinted with that same sorrow and longing. "These models, the ones the magazines airbrush to look even thinner than they are? They are on the way out." I noted then a lineup of models had replaced the first and found my eyes widening at the comparison. Still tall and slender, but muscular, a bit heavier in the body, without the prominent bone protrusions. Yes, they were still skinny by normal standards—hey, I was a very fit size eight, thanks, and didn't feel the need to starve myself down to an impossible number that just made me feel bad about myself—but they had a robustness to them the previous lineup didn't possess. As if someone had sucked the souls out of the initial group but these young men and women held onto theirs.

Not a fair comparison and I wasn't judging or anything. But seriously. Hamburgers and chocolate chip cookies all around.

"The new rules in France restrict underweight models," Vivian said, nodding to the slinking strides of the second group. "And Grace has seized on that, made it endemic of her entire line. Henry, on the other hand, refuses to accept the way things are going." It was obvious whose side Vivian was on.

"Up-and-coming designers and models need better guidelines and our," yes, she said "our" like she still belonged, "industry needs smart, beautiful and talented representatives. Yes, they are still thin," she shrugged like that was a necessary evil, "but they are fit, strong, impressive. More like warriors than victims." Huh, interesting way to look at it. Hey, I wasn't the one speaking up, and since Vivian had a horse in that race, I figured I'd keep my mouth shut and let her vent. "Grace's models are all vocal about education, most of them in college for science, technology, engineering." How interesting. "She handpicks them to ensure they are equally brilliant and beautiful. It's a fascinating approach and really adds to the integrity of her clothing line."

"That's amazing," I said, blurting it out but meaning it.

Why then did Vivian look so annoyed by my attitude? "We're not all dumb blondes," she snapped. Before I could reassure her I didn't think anything of the sort, she spun and walked away, that characteristic runway strut in evidence in her stride.

And I had to admit I felt bad she'd left thinking I was judging her. I guess my animosity was really easing up after all.

I turned back, doing my best not to feel self-conscious about myself while arguing in my head that I was perfect the way I was. Crew wasn't complaining, after all, and I was the fittest I'd been in my life, partially thanks to him and our workouts. But it was hard after a while to keep up my internal "I'm awesome!" dialogue in the face of all that skinny beauty parading past me like I was on the outside of perfection and if I could maybe just lose ten more pounds, I could be one of the cool kids…

Faith's appearance caught my attention, if only because I had such a bad taste in my mouth left over from our unnecessary confrontation. The blonde strutted with excessive aggression, taking focus from every other person on the stage. Kami strode behind her, face twisted into a bitter little frown, aimed directly at Faith's back, the flat expression the other models wore nowhere in evidence on either of them. Whatever their disagreement, when Faith did her turn at the end of the catwalk and spun to stride past Kami, they exchanged a low word between them, a moment of anger, that made the dark-haired model's face flash into rage, while Faith tossed her blonde hair over her shoulder as if she'd won whatever argument they'd been having with that single exchange.

And in that moment, I released my secret wish I could be one of them and exhaled, grateful for the life I lived that had nothing to do with bitterness, vindictive co-workers or the need to be perfect weighing on my shoulders.

I spotted Jill and joined her, feeling her tension as I did but smiling so she'd know I wasn't about to give her a hard time over moonlighting. She flashed her own quick smile, relaxing somewhat, though she stayed at attention in her dark suit. I'd never seen her dressed like this before, so used to her in her deputy's uniform it felt odd, almost surreal as if she'd run off and joined the feds or something.

"How's Matt?" I spotted him across the staging area and waved. He waved back before tucking his hands behind him and resuming his own serious pose.

"Bruised." Jill snorted, not exactly lady-like but totally her. Hey, was she wearing makeup? And her ponytail had marks of curls at the ends rather than her usual pin-straight and no-nonsense look. Was someone trying to fit in with the fashion set? "He'll survive."

"I bet," I said. "How's the job going?"

She glanced sideways at me before shrugging. "Which one?"

I laughed so she'd know I had nothing against this sideline. "Both," I said. "Your day job is hard enough, dealing with Robert." I eye-rolled while she seemed to flinch at the mention then looked away. Huh, usually I could get at least a bit of a sigh or an agreement out of her when it came to my cousin. Could he have had something to do with her comment yesterday morning? She was pretty uptight if she couldn't even muster a groan of misery. "As for this lot, I think they're more dangerous to each other than any outside threat."

Jill did laugh at that. "Tell me about it," she said, keeping her voice down but leaning into me. "If I have to break up one more catfight I'm going to scream."

"I'm feeling a bit schleppy in their company," I

said, tugging at the hem of my t-shirt. I'd worn it and jeans and sneakers for the morning, knowing I'd be working with Mom and discarding the apron she'd given me before coming here to be nosy.

"You and me both," Jill said, almost sad. "I've never been, you know, like that." She glanced at Matt who seemed intent on the models. Too intent? "Maybe I should take some lessons."

I poked her in the ribs. "If he can't appreciate who he has, he's not worthy of you."

She shook her head, flashed a weak smile. "That's not it," she said. Then fell suddenly silent, like she wanted to say something else but couldn't muster the words.

Well, fine then. "I'd like to see one of them take down a criminal with their bare hands," I said. "You're amazing, Jill. Don't ever forget it."

She didn't comment, but she did smile again, and I left her with what encouragement I could. If there was one thing I knew, it was internal dialogue wasn't something another person could shift. If she wanted to beat herself up or doubt or fall down the rabbit hole of poor me, there was nothing I—or anyone else—could do to stop her.

I just hoped she didn't let it go on too long. Or that it was a mistake to not ask more pointed questions about her friendship statement at the end of yesterday's class. I figured, though, if Jill wanted to talk, she'd talk. Right?

As for me, it was time to shed my own defeating thoughts and get myself home to Petunia's. Mom had the rest of the day well in hand and I had a bed and breakfast to run. With my mind focused on the paperwork I had to tackle sometime today, I almost missed the familiar form of the silver-haired man who hurried through the lobby of the lodge, head down, shoulders rounded as he barreled into me like he didn't even see me.

"Malcolm!"

CHAPTER TEN

He flinched when I said his name, stopped dead and stared into my eyes, his own green ones empty and hurt. I gasped softly at the sight of him, his face sunken, dark circles adding depth to his gaze, his jaw shining with a few days' beard growth. Even his clothing seemed out of sorts, unkempt like he'd slept in them, his normally tidy silver hair askew on one side. But it was the haunted look on his face, how his lower lip shuddered just a fraction as his hands grasped my upper arms a bit too tight that made me worry about him.

Yes, he was a criminal mob boss, at least according to my dad. And I'd had enough interaction with him and his boys at The Orange to know he wasn't on the up-and-up most days. But ever since we'd met, since he'd done his best to pull me into the mystery of Siobhan Doyle and my father's connection to that mystery, I'd felt an odd affinity for Malcolm Murray, one that deepened as my concern for his state of mind grew at the sight of him after he'd been missing from Reading for months.

Before I could ask him where he'd been or what was going on, he pushed me away from him, releasing me as quickly as he'd grasped onto me. I staggered, not from the force of his motion but from surprise and gaped as he strode past me. I reacted without thinking, grasping for the elbow of his jacket, pulling him to a stop.

"Malcolm," I said, "where have you been?"

He shook his head, tried to pull free, lips working but not saying anything.

"Where is Siobhan?" I had a horrible feeling, one that appeared when he'd vanished, when I failed to reach the older woman I'd only spoken to once on the phone from across the Atlantic. She'd told me she was coming to Reading, that she had affairs to put in order, that what she had to tell me had to be said in person. Frustrating as that was, I was used to it when it came to this particular situation. After all, my own father wouldn't even talk about Siobhan or Malcolm and insisted I stay out of whatever linked their past to his.

Like that would get him anywhere.

Malcolm's face crumpled at the mention of her name and for a moment I feared the worst. When he finally spoke, his voice cracked, his accent harsher than usual. "At home, in Ireland."

"You went to see her." He nodded, though that much was obvious. "She said she wanted to talk to me in person. Malcolm, I need to know what's going on."

Whatever willingness he felt to fill me in further died as he caught sight of someone across the lobby. But when I looked up, following his gaze, I couldn't tell who his target was, there were so many people milling around. He pulled free at last, scowling at the floor, no longer meeting my eyes.

"I have other business, lass," he said. Paused, inhaled, exhaled a shaky breath before finally looking up and meeting my gaze, his green eyes rimmed in moisture. I wasn't expecting such a display of emotion from him and found myself responding, my hand going out to his arm, my throat tight as matching sorrow answered though I had no idea what made him so upset. "Maybe your da, he's right, Fee." What? Since when? "Maybe the past, it needs to stay in the past. For all our sakes." And, with that, he walked away, hands in his pockets, shoulders bowed. Not the man I knew at all.

Making me even more determined to find out just what it was he and my father were hiding.

I checked in with Mom briefly but didn't linger, heading out and into the back hallway, head down, still thinking about Malcolm and that particularly lingering headache. Why did new shiny mysteries (like Alicia and Jared and Jill) always seem to take precedence to the ones that I really needed answers to (like Siobhan and the Reading horde and the Pattersons and Blackstone)? Seriously, my brain needed some kind of priority overhaul, because when I wasn't pondering something that had nothing to do with me, I was on autopilot and nothing got in outside the mundane of my day-to-day.

Funny how being distracted seemed to be getting me into trouble today. When I exited the kitchen and made my way down the hall, I was walking at a good enough clip that when the tall, handsome—if older—gentleman leaving the men's facilities made his presence physically known I didn't have time to stop and instead ran right into him. Frederick Newmark's initial sneering reaction turned to a sort of vile little grin of appreciation that gave me the instant heebies while he looked me over, big hands grasping my upper arms where they'd risen to catch me. Thing was, he didn't immediately let me go, leering—yes, leering openly, the old reprobate—down the front of my t-shirt. I pulled away, blushing as I realized the normally modest top had stretched at the V-neck, likely thanks to lugging flats of water bottles, exposing the curve of my bra. I hastily rectified the situation, wondering what was going on with me today that I had more confrontations to deal with than not, a personal record.

"Has anyone ever told you that you could be a model?" He winked at me, pale eyes narrowed, fake tan barely hiding his advancing age, some kind of procedure to tighten his skin making him look like he'd been stretched just a bit too thin. He raised one hand again, a diamond ring flashing on his middle finger, and I dodged it, unable to stop the scowl of *ew, gross* that crossed my face.

"Seriously?" I huffed and moved on, doing my best to ignore the teensy tiny little thrill of maybe I could have been someone that his words roused in me while mentally kicking the girl within who needed such validation.

In the car on the way home I had to admit, even yucked out by him, his question had an impact on me. And I was old enough to know better, successful and in love. What kind of sway would he have over someone less put together? Because, hello, I was put together.

Yeah, okay, Fee. Sure.

At home, I shrugged off the weird encounter and headed down to my apartment with my pug huffing her way on my heels to the kitchen. I immediately called Siobhan's number again but ran into the same problem I'd had so many times before.

"We're sorry," the recorded voice said, "but the mailbox for the number you've dialed is full. Please hang up and try again."

Heart heavy, knowing there wasn't anything else I could do, I dove into paperwork and Petunia's and did my best to put it out of my mind.

Funny thing, right? The harder you try to forget about something, usually the more it surfaces until it's about to drive you bonkers. I sighed over a paragraph I'd tried to read at least four times before sitting back and closing the internet browser, not really caring about shifts in tax law at the moment while my worry about Siobhan and Malcolm's change in attitude weighed on my mind.

I was just about to dial Dad and demand answers—surely, he'd come to his senses if I pushed him hard enough (right, Fee, because you would and you were just like your dad, silly goose)—when my phone rang of its own accord. I squeaked out a mouse-like protest, realizing I'd been staring at the thing as if it were a snake about to bite me, letting out a little snort of amusement at my own reaction while I answered the familiar number.

Alicia didn't give me time to say hello. The moment I tapped the green receiver button, her panicked voice shrieked my name on the other end of the line.

"FEE! I need you at the lodge. NOW!" She promptly hung up.

No further attempts to reach her made it through. I glanced outside at the darkness, tucking into my down jacket, wondering if I needed to call Crew but sighing and heading out with a quick wave for Daisy who let me go without questions. Whatever the disaster, I was sure I could handle it at 7PM at night. Alicia did tend toward the hysterical from time to time, bless her heart. If there was some kind of drama with the fashion show, I wasn't sure I was the best person to help her, but she was my friend, and I was willing to give it a go.

Back door.

I caught that text as I parked and, frowning at

Alicia's cryptic message, hurried around to the rear entrance near the ski lift. She met me there, shaking, eyes huge, hands grasping me and jerking me inside before she slammed the big door shut. The hall lights were out for some reason and when I opened my mouth to ask her what was going on, she instead yanked on me, pulling me through the side door and into the staging area for the fashion show. The large dining room had been converted into seating with the central catwalk taking up the center. I stopped at the edge of the chairs, confused and now very worried while Alicia's face, pale and panicked, glowed under the faint lights of the emergency lamps overhead.

What happened to the main lighting? Was this the emergency she needed help with? I wasn't sure what I could do to—

My gaze caught movement over Alicia's shoulder, and I froze, trying to identify the object while my heart skipped but my brain sighed a long and bitter oh no way, come on, really?

Something swung from the ceiling, something long and slim with blonde hair, dressed in a gown and giant silver shoes, something that looked far too much like the dead body of Faith Leeman to be anything else.

Alicia chose that moment to take a deep breath. And scream like she'd been waiting this whole time, for my arrival and support, to let it out.

CHAPTER ELEVEN

"Well," I said, trying for cheerful as my boyfriend's face settled into the familiar scowl he wore when I came into close proximity of a dead body, "at least I wasn't the one who found it this time, right?"

Crew didn't comment, focusing instead, it seemed, on breathing slowly and patiently, bless him. "Tell me everything," he said, that graveled depth of tone just as familiar, though I had to admit I found it sexier than usual, rather than irritating like I used to. He loved me, didn't he? I could afford to relax a bit.

Alicia hovered next to me, hand grasping mine tightly, face pale save for two bright pink spots on the points of her cheeks and mottled down her neck and décolletage. Hey, I'd been there, no way was I judging her visceral reaction to finding Faith Leeman hanging from the ceiling.

At least she hadn't had to deal with being pressed up against the woman's body, had she? Not like my run-in at *Zip It!*. Comparing deaths was equal parts disturbing and natural at this point, something I wasn't sure I wanted to share with Crew.

"Can you tell me," the sheriff said with the faint tick under his eye bouncing, proof he wasn't happy about the present situation while Dr. Aberstock oversaw the slow lowering of the dead model's body onto the tarp he'd laid out on the catwalk. I tried to ignore the slow swaying of her limp form, the way she turned on the scraps of fabric twisted around her neck, how the creaking of the pipe overhead made my heart leap at each moaning protest. At least the scaffolding held, so kudos to the crew who put the stage together, and the tall ladder was easy access, so whether suicide—unlikely—or murder—my gut screamed that was the case—it had been likely easy enough for whoever did this to gain access to the means to hang her.

Which meant someone strong. So, a man? One of the designers, possibly? Or two women, even. Kami had clearly shown animosity. She could have had help.

Not that it was right or anything, but I had this habit of guessing.

I didn't breathe a sigh of relief until the body touched the stage. Meanwhile, Crew had finished his sentence and I almost missed it. "Why is it, Ms.

Conway, you decided to call Fee instead of the sheriff's department when you discovered the body?"

Ah. That's why he was upset. Well, I could hardly blame him. And I really should have asked that question myself. Pretty telling, I guess, that wondering why Alicia brought me in before Crew hadn't even crossed my mind. That's what I got for being the center of the murder scene here in Reading.

"I'm sorry, sheriff," Alicia said, teeth chattering, her hand so tight around mine I winced a bit at the pressure but didn't let her go. "I panicked. I've never had to deal with anything like this before and all I could think of was Fee had so I called her, and she came right away and I'm so... so... glad." She stumbled to a halt after blurting her way through that run-on statement, inhaling and letting out a wail at the end that turned into sobs before she spun into my shoulder and clung to me like she'd fall over if I didn't hold her up.

Crew's annoyance faded instantly, and he eye-rolled at me before sighing out his visible frustration. "It's going to be all right," he said, soothing tone not really helping but at least he tried. "Can you tell me, did you touch anything?"

She shook her head, not looking as Dr. Aberstock began his examination while I couldn't help but stare. Hard to see anything in detail from this distance, though. I'd be asking questions in short order if only to irritate his young intern, Barry Clements. I'd thought Barry had been employed temporarily, as part of his education, but it turned out he'd chosen to stick around, rumors about financial issues and tuition reaching me without my having to dig for them. I felt for him, if that was the case. But he'd been less than helpful when I'd faced the death of Grayson Gallinger, toeing the Patterson company line when Geoffrey Jenkins was in favor, and he hadn't done much to endear himself to me since. If anything, the young man I'd first thought rather likable had turned bitter and resentful, and I wondered if it was his natural inclination, his loss of funding for school or pressure he might still be receiving from those who would prefer I stayed out of the loop.

Right, Fee, because everything that happened in Reading was about you. Snort.

Jill glared from the side of the stage, arms crossed over her chest, staying out of the way, about as perplexing as the dead body. She'd looked so furious when she'd found me with Alicia, Crew's arrival drawing her attention, I was sure she was going to say something. Instead, she'd backed off and just stood in that same spot for the last fifteen minutes. Weird, though Crew didn't comment that his deputy wasn't stepping in to help and I wondered what was going on between them that put any kind of wedge with Crew on one side and the usually amiable Jill on the other.

"Where is she?" I heard Jared's voice before I saw him, the sound having an immediate effect on her. She spun away from me and abandoned her grip on my hand like I never existed, rushing to her fiancé who engulfed her in his arms. Hey, hang on. Was he actually scowling at me like this was my fault or something?

Crew spoke before I could be annoyed enough to say anything. "I'll have more questions for Ms. Conway," he said. "But they can wait until she's feeling more herself." That really was nice of him, though Jared just nodded and looked down at her, rocking her a little and whispering to her. I let go of my own irritation at his reaction, knowing he was just responding to her hurt and fear. Still, sheesh. I came running when she needed me. Jared could let up just a little bit.

As for Jill, the moment Jared led Alicia away, she finally approached, Matt lingering behind her, his scowl matching hers. And though Crew was her boss and she really needed to be addressing him right now, helping with the investigation, it was me she had words for.

To my utter shock, she hissed in my face, anger so openly apparent I gasped. "What the hell were you thinking? You should have come and got me."

She said *what*? Crew's hand settled on her shoulder, but she shrugged him off like he offended her. Their eyes met with the kind of mistrustful animosity that enemies held for each other, the realization I'd missed something important hitting me like a blow.

"Fee did the right thing," he said, voice low and mild. "She called the police, Jill. And while you're a deputy,"—wow, why did it sound like he wanted to add *for now* to that as a caveat?—"you weren't working in that capacity at the time."

She didn't respond, jaw set, eyes flat and angry. Matt looked uncomfortable though not nearly as upset as she did, more like he just wanted this to go away, would have liked to lead Jill off somewhere and put an end to the brewing fight. Because, yup, a fight was brewing, boiling under the surface while I gaped back and forth between my boyfriend and my friend and wondered what was going on that put them at odds.

"Now," Crew said, still softly but with that particular weight to his words I was familiar enough with, the old FBI commanding tone in full force, "if you'd like to change into your uniform, I'm happy to have you help investigate this case. Or, if you'd prefer to continue your private work, I'll ask you to secure the perimeter and keep everyone out so I can do my job."

Jill's nostrils flared. For a long moment, I was sure she was going to argue. Instead, finally, with a sharp nod, she turned away and stormed past Matt who shrugged an apology before following her. Crew watched her go with sadness in his eyes, then sighed and met my gaze with a small head shake.

"Not now," he said, "please. We can talk about it later." His hand slid down my arm, fingers squeezing mine before letting me go. "Are you okay?"

There was the kindness and compassion I'd been hoping for. But now I knew his annoyance wasn't just with Alicia and finding me here. He had more issues to deal with, work issues he'd been keeping from me. I reached out and mimicked his movement, releasing his hand after a brief, comforting touch.

"I'm fine," I said. "What's a dead body between friends?"

He actually smiled, though it was tired. "Go home, Fee," he said. "This one's mine."

I wanted to hug him, but I knew better. Not that he wasn't demonstrative, but we had an agreement about kissing at the office, and I assumed hugging at a crime scene fell under that set of rules. Besides, the last thing I wanted was to make him uncomfortable when he had a murder to investigate.

Oh, yes. Again, sure, it could have been suicide. Except that there was no way Faith could have hung herself unless she could fly. Or move the ladder on her own. So, I was calling this one without hearing from the doc or the crime scene techs right now checking that same ladder for fingerprints.

I left, offering a back pat for Alicia who snuffled against Jared's shoulder, relenting when he reached out to hug me against the two of them in apology for his initial reaction.

"Thank you," he whispered, letting me go. I just nodded and walked on, determined to hunt for Jill and Matt and grill my friends about her confrontation with Crew. But from the way Jill, head down and hands at her hips, shook her head while Matt talked fast and low to her, she was in no mood to chat. I could have forced a conversation, but I opted instead for the smart route for once and went home.

Look at me being all thoughtful and everything. That was, until she calmed down. Then I'd be cornering her and firing her up again. Honestly, my choice to leave wasn't really for Jill's benefit, anyway. Whatever her problem was, I left to save Crew from having to deal with his deputy yelling at his girlfriend when I gave her a hard time for being mean to him for no reason.

Then again, did she have a reason? I thought it out as I drove home to Petunia's, the short trip down the mountain picturesque as a postcard but utterly lost on me, thanks to my internal turmoil. This had to be a new thing, right? I would have noticed. Or would I? I'd been so lost in Crew and in Petunia's and the annex, in this year's unwinding business, had I failed to see something that had been brewing a while?

No, no way. Had to be current. Which meant it might just blow over without my interference. On the other hand, it could turn into something that lead to Jill leaving Reading, something that I'd feared when Crew's job was at risk, not when he was firmly back on the bright side of the good folks of our little slice of America.

Whatever the case, and whatever their issue, I'd get it out of Crew now that I knew something was up.

I parked in the lot between the annex and the main house, my personal spot marked with the hand-painted cutout of a pug illuminated in my headlights,

Fiona Fleming in black across her round tummy. The space markers had been Daisy's idea and while a bit chintzy had an equally cute appeal I finally went along with. At least having the lot kept us from running into parking violations, though the occasional indiscretion still meant I had to deal with town hall more often than I liked. Whoever was behind the rabid enforcement of all things parking (Robert, I'm looking at you), things had only gotten worse over the years.

It wasn't until I entered through the back door and into the kitchen, I realized Mom hadn't gone home yet and, better yet, Dad was there. Wherever he'd stashed his pickup truck, it wasn't in the lot, and I winced, wondering if he'd found a new way to piss off my cousin with his choice in parking spots. Dad's office was just down the street from town hall and he took full advantage of the lot there, something that Robert detested and tried to use against my father. Only to run up against Olivia's irritation and continual support of my dad. It had been a delightful winter of my dad contesting tickets and Robert doing his very best to get Dad's truck towed. While I'm sure my father was amusing himself with the whole issue, I was getting a bit tired of Petunia's being a focus of attention as Robert's attempts to retaliate against Dad meant him hovering outside my place looking for violations to write up.

Grunt, growl and bother.

I greeted my father with a knowing frown, though he engulfed me in a hug rather than commenting on my expression.

"What is it with you and dead bodies?" He looked down at me as he released me, the familiar scent of the laundry detergent Mom used lingering on his checkered shirt, his eyes narrowed with worry. I'd always looked up to my dad, his bravery, his stoic strength, how he always took everything in stride. Except when it came to me and Mom, I finally realized. He felt far more deeply than my former sheriff turned P.I. tough-guy father would ever admit.

"Alicia found her," I said. "Not me this time."

He nodded, let me go, Mom hugging me in turn. She, at least, never failed to show her concern, touching my hair, my cheeks, before releasing me. The lingering scent of her favorite stew recipe she'd served for dinner filled the kitchen with the comforting aroma of beef, fresh biscuits and childhood.

I told them both what I learned, unsurprised my father knew most of what I did already.

"The doc," Dad said with a shrug and a grin. "And I'm way ahead of Crew on this one. I already have a suspect."

"You could call him and let him know." That wasn't a request, though from the crinkling around Dad's eyes, the way he fought a grin, he wasn't about to let my boyfriend have the information he'd uncovered that easily. Made me wonder about their relationship. Dad had been in cahoots with Crew on a number of occasions in the last year or so, though neither of them would tell me what they were working on together. Should have made me nervous, maybe. Instead, I just sighed and carried on.

Except, in light of Jill's response to Crew, I felt anger surface for the first time in a while and let Dad have it.

"You know," I snapped, "we're supposed to be working together. That's hard to do when you keep things to yourself."

Instead of responding with his own temper, though, he booped me on the nose and winked. "When you're ready to commit," Dad said in that infuriatingly calm and level tone that made me want to smack him, "you let me know, Fee."

Dads.

CHAPTER TWELVE

He was lucky he changed the subject. "You're aware Mila Martin is back in town?"

Mom looked worried enough I shrugged. "I know, Dad. She's staying here."

Dad flinched at that, Mom's reaction enough that I paid attention.

"That girl is a stalker freak." Wow, Dad, nice. Not. "You need to be careful around her, Fee. She's been in a mental institution, court-enforced."

"I'm aware of that," I said. "She told me."

Mom glanced at Dad then at me, biting her lower lip. "Do you think she's a threat?"

"I think she's here for Grace." I hated to tell Mom that, considering she was all about Vivian these days. Dad inhaled like he wanted to argue, but fell silent, Mom staring, as the kitchen door swung shut, the devil we spoke of watching us like she'd been there all along.

There was no way she could have missed what we were saying, but Mila didn't seem put off by the fact.

"Fee, I'm so happy you're back." She completely ignored my parents, gesturing for me to join her at the door. I hesitated a moment, but Mila's nervous expression made me relent. I left Mom and Dad who stayed quiet, tense, and joined the young woman, a bit surprised and creeped out when she took my hand and led me out of the kitchen and earshot of my parents.

When she tucked me into the quiet dining room, dinner long over, the space dark and still, I almost resisted, but Mila's furtive glances caught and held my curiosity.

"Can I help you with something?" Weird, yes, but hardly threatening.

Her big eyes locked on my face once I spoke. Mila's lower lip trembled, her hand on mine cold and clammy, as she pressed something into my fingers and closed them around it. I glanced down at what looked like a piece of paper with writing just visible through the folded edges as Mila spoke.

"I found this," she whispered loudly enough it was apparent she hadn't brought all of her marbles out of the hospital with her. "It might help you in your investigation."

Did everyone in Reading know about the murder? "I'm not part of the case," I said. "That's

Crew's job."

She nodded slowly, eyes massive and staring. "You'll find the murderer," she said. "I know it. I have faith in you, Fiona. You're the best, the absolute best. Anyone would want you working their murder. I'd want you working mine."

Um, okies, not freaking out or anything. I unfolded the paper, realizing it was torn and pieced back together. No, wait, not torn. This had been shredded by a machine. I looked up again, met Mila's eyes. "Where did you get this?" Okay, so just because it was likely she'd stolen this from somewhere she shouldn't have been didn't mean I wasn't going to read it. Because yeah. I was going to read it. And did so, skimming the contents while Mila leaned closer. Close enough I could smell the faint mustiness from her sweater, the generic scent of her shampoo, feel her hot breath on my cheek. Eep.

"That ex-model, Noel." Mila's voice had a dreamy tone to it suddenly, her lips in a soft smile, eyes moist, unblinking. "I had a look around her room earlier. This was in the trash."

Okay, that wasn't a good thing. How many other guest's rooms had she broken into? Before I could mention she'd likely be getting a visit from Crew in the next little bit, Mila let me go and hugged herself, beaming at me.

"You're welcome, Fee," she said before turning and drifting away, glancing back at me a few times as she retreated toward the foyer and the stairs. I let her go, not because I condoned what she'd done, but knowing that Dad was right, and it was probably for the best Crew dealt with the poor unfortunate young woman.

As for the stolen, repaired note, well. I'd hand it over to my boyfriend after a quick read-through of the contents, wouldn't I? Like a good Fiona Fleming.

The tape Mila used made it hard to read in low light and I stepped out into the better illumination of the foyer just as the front door slammed open and a furious and agitated Vivian French stormed in. I'd seen her upset a few times in the past, worked up, but typically that had been cold and icy, the Queen of Wheat having a hissy fit. The only time I'd really seen her temper was the day we'd stood outside the back of her bakery and screamed at each other like a pair of spitting cats, venting on each other though neither of us really was to blame for our upset.

This Vivian, however, was clearly emotionally invested in her fury, stomping to a halt next to me with the sort of aggressive agitation I usually equated with myself, not her, no sign of her normal collected and crisp vitriol in sight.

"What exactly are you doing here?" She grasped my arm and tugged on me like she planned to physically remove me from the premises and relocate me where it was she thought I should be at that moment. "You're supposed to be at the lodge solving the murder."

Um, what? "I'm not a deputy, Vivian." She was well aware of that fact.

She snorted, so uncharacteristic I couldn't

respond right away. That was fine, she did it for me. "Like that's ever stopped you before," she snarled. "Now, get back there and find out who killed Faith before this impacts Grace's business."

Ah. Gotcha. "Vivian," I said, "Crew's handling it. He's a great sheriff. We both know I just get in the way and make things harder for him." Okay, I hadn't meant to say that out loud and fully expected her to turn to disdain and agree.

Instead, to my utter shock, she crumbled, her face showing fear, sorrow, not a trace of the anger that carried her into my foyer remaining as she clutched at my arm, tears standing in her pale, blue eyes. For the first time since I'd met Vivian, I saw her, really saw her, the woman behind the mask of derision and control and my heart broke.

"Please, Fee," she said, voice cracking, a tear tracing down her cheek, marring her perfect makeup while I stared in surprise and unexpected but engulfing compassion, "you have to help. I'm begging you. Grace can't be touched by this. She just can't."

I fish lipped, I'm not too proud to admit it, while Vivian pulled herself under control. But her open worry didn't shift, and nor did she try to hide her concern for the designer as she went on.

"I know we've never been friends." She released me, dabbing delicately at the tear on her face, shaking her head, inhaling and exhaling before continuing. "But please, for Grace. This could ruin her whole season if she's tied to the murder."

What did Vivian know that I didn't? "Is she a suspect?"

She shrugged, delicate and rather fragile inside her designer suit, looking the frailest, the most lost I'd ever seen her. It was my turn to reach for her and I did, taking her elbow in one hand. She didn't fight my touch but also didn't collapse as I feared she might. What was her relationship to Grace that she had such a powerful reaction to the woman's plight? A plight that I had as yet to even confirm? Or did Vivian know full well her friend was a suspect, might even be the murderer, and that was her motivation for coming to me?

Vivian had to know if Grace did it, if she killed Faith, I wouldn't protect her even if I did like her as much as was already obvious. But, as the Queen of Wheat visibly strengthened, I realized I actually didn't care if Grace was guilty or not. Because for me this wasn't about the designer I'd come to admire and like.

"Not for Grace," I said softly, surprising myself. "For you, Vivian. For what you did for Mom." Well, that was the excuse. Sheesh, had I really gone soft on my dislike for my old foe? I guess so.

She shook her head, though her old animosity and coldness didn't come back. "Lucy has always been good to me. Kind. I couldn't let them ruin her."

So, she *had* been the source of my mother's renewed confidence. I'd know it intellectually, but it was nice to have confirmation from the monarch's mouth.

"I'll do what I can." Oh, Fee. "No promises. And Vivian, if Grace is guilty…"

She swallowed, wouldn't meet my eyes. "If she's guilty, Fee, she needs to be punished. But if she isn't… if she's accused of Faith's murder, this could ruin her." She finally looked up, blue eyes so open I wondered how I'd ever disliked or misjudged her. "Thank you." Vivian gently freed herself from my grip and backed away, touching her cheek, her hair, smoothing the front of her suit. "Your best is all I ask."

All I could do was watch as she spun then and left, closing the door far more softly behind her than she'd entered, conflicting emotions at war inside me while I wondered how I was going to explain my nosiness to Crew in a way he'd understand.

CHAPTER THIRTEEN

I returned my attention to the note to distract myself from the inevitable confrontation with my sheriff boyfriend, though just reading the patched-together scraps of shredded paper meant I was taking steps that would likely end in him grinding his teeth and sighing a lot. Oh well, I could live with him being annoyed with me and figured at some point he'd be asking me for input anyway, right?

I skimmed the contents, taking in the gist if not the full details the first time through. Apparently, Noel had concerns about Faith, though the bulk of the contents was missing. When I forced my eyes to slow down and read what Mila had managed to fit in some semblance of order, it read:

You have to, Henry—her usual tricks—just listen for

once—Faith's plans to—pay attention this—Noel.

I frowned at the missing parts, realizing Mila must have only retrieved portions of the note and, when I flipped it over, understood the lack of connective tissue. She'd taken the bits she'd found and carefully and completely taped them down to a fresh piece of paper, creating a solid backing for what little remained. And while there wasn't much to go on, it was suspicious enough that when the front door opened at the exact moment I frowned my way through trying to figure out who to talk to first, I almost pounced on the very woman who had written this particular note in the first place.

She seemed shocked by my sudden approach, and I did my best to dial back my enthusiasm just before I blurted out a demand she tell me what it was she had against Faith. In fact, her reaction actually gave me the moment I needed to double-take and check myself before I could put myself in a position to be accused of breaking into her room and stealing her things. Because I hadn't, after all. I was just taking advantage of Mila's misappropriation of information. That didn't make me a bad person.

It didn't.

"Ms. Fleming." Noel paused, staring at me, her face pale, dark circles even more pronounced as she looked at me as if I were going to bring her harm. "Are you all right?"

Whoops. "Fine," I said, tugging hard on my curiosity. I must have seemed downright dangerous for her to ask me like that.

Instead, she softened just slightly, hesitating before speaking again with compassion in her voice. "I heard you were there. When they found Faith."

Ah, that was what she meant. I nodded, mind spinning to find a way to use that moment of her weakness to my advantage. "Poor thing," I said. "I'm sure they'll find who did it."

Noel flinched and her ranking in my suspect pool notched up a place or two. "I'm sure they will." She swallowed, the uncomfortable silence between us growing. Now, my father taught me if you wanted someone to tell you information, but they weren't super forthcoming you should always stay quiet. The guilty hated a vacuum, and I don't mean the floor cleaning variety. Weight on a conscience had a way of blurting itself out through the lips of those who had secrets to keep, and I'd used this technique in the past with great results.

This time, though? Nada. Zippo zilcheroonie. So, either Noel had nothing to do with Faith's death or she didn't feel guilty for killing her. I had a hard time believing the woman was that icy cold, especially with fear showing behind her big eyes. Just like I struggled to believe someone her size could wrangle even Faith's slim body up a ladder to hang her. Then again, fear and rage gave us the sort of strength we wouldn't normally command and, to be honest, while Noel looked skinny and weak, she could have been much stronger than she appeared.

When she shifted as if to go, the tension between us at the kind of height that meant she was going to beat a retreat, I offered up the scraps of note, showing her the pieces taped together. She frowned this time, anger surfacing, and when she met my gaze, hers was shadowed, darkened.

"Where did you get that?" She didn't try to defend herself, came across instead as indignant and professional.

"In your trash," I said. "While I was cleaning your room." Yeah, little white lie, Fee. Nice job. "I saw Faith's name and, naturally, it made me wonder. Considering you threw this out, Noel, I've done nothing wrong."

She looked like she wanted to argue but shrugged instead, thin shoulders working under the heavy wool of her wrap. Despite the thickness of the fabric, I could still make out the hard lines of her bones protruding through her skin as if someone stretched her far too thin for her own good. "It's hardly a secret I've had issues with Faith Leeman."

If she said so. "Were you at the lodge when she was killed?"

Noel's frown didn't fade. "I don't have to answer that," she said. "Good night, Ms. Fleming."

Yeah, I could have followed her, poked and prodded her further. Almost did. Except, while I stood there considering that course of action, I was interrupted. And not in a nice way. In a jump out of my skin and shriek like a little girl way.

"I think she killed that girl." Mila had somehow appeared behind me, leaning over my shoulder, staring at the now empty staircase with those huge, wide eyes of hers. What the actual *what?* I'd thought she'd gone back up to her room. Where had she been hiding? I caught at my throat with one hand, gasping for a breath, shaking a bit from the shock of her sudden appearance. Mila didn't seem to notice she'd upset me, head tilting to one side like a dog listening for a distant sound only she could hear. "I've been watching her." Her head turned on a slow swivel, eyes meeting mine in that glazed and staring way that was really starting to freak me out. "There's something wrong with her, Fee."

Pots and kettles, Mila.

"I'm sure the sheriff will be happy to have this." I backed out of the young woman's space, though she drifted after me, keeping the distance the same as before, a magnet on an unerring trajectory and for the first time I actually had a worried thought. Then shrugged it off and tried a smile. "Meanwhile, I'm going to have to ask you not to break into other guest's rooms." Wow, did I just say that? She didn't know I was going to tell Crew. But she had to understand I didn't condone her activity.

Mila shrugged, dreamy smile responding to my weak and worried one. "If you say so, Fee." She hugged me suddenly but let me go when I squeaked in shock, drifting away like she knew I'd had my limit of her attention. She climbed the stairs for real this time, again leaving me to wonder where she'd gone if not up to her room earlier, shuddering to think she'd lingered in some unseen place, watching me. And again that thought perhaps she wasn't here for Grace crossed my mind.

Crushed in relief as the front door opened and tall, dark and divinely delicious walked through.

CHAPTER FOURTEEN

It was inevitable we ended up downstairs in my apartment, Crew with a beer in one hand, me pondering the uncomfortable quiet that he settled in when I told him about Mila's snooping. He examined the note before sighing and setting it aside.

"I'm going to have to talk to her," he said.

I nodded. "I know." Why did I feel protective of her, anyway? She'd stalked Willow mercilessly, though I'd felt sorry for Mila since we'd met and despite her following the star around, she'd never done any actual harm. But she could hurt my business with her illegal activity. I really needed to go upstairs and kick her out right now. That's why my feet felt glued to the floor.

Crew took a long drink before setting down his

bottle with a soft glass on tile thud, staring at the rim with those serious blue eyes, bangs growing out just enough I felt the itch to just reach out and push his hair back, so I had an excuse to touch him. Fee. *Focus.*

"I'll see what else I can dig up about Noel," he said. Wait, what else? He was already on to her? "After I have a chat with your nosy guest." He laughed then, soft and low and graveled, my favorite, before leaning forward and tugging me toward him, tucking me in between his knees, free hand on the small of my back, eyes level with mine where he perched on the stool at the counter. "If I arrested everyone in town for nosiness, I wouldn't have a girlfriend."

Smartypants. "Are you okay with me helping?" I didn't mean for that to come out in a little girl voice and cleared my throat before trying again with a bit more force behind my words. "Vivian doesn't like taking no for an answer."

"And you care oh so much about what Vivian French wants, right?" Crew's humor didn't fade. "It has nothing to do with the fact you can't stand that someone else came across a dead body and you had to find out secondhand."

Grumph. Now he was just being snarky.

"Like I'd be able to stop you," he said, not even sighing like he usually did. "Just be careful. Scratch that." He shook his head, the ends of his black hair just starting to curl from length shining as he did. Growl. He was so deliciously distracting. Dead body?

What dead body? "How about you keep me in the loop, and we'll worry about the rest if and when someone tries to kill you."

Okay, he sounded reasonable enough, but there was tightness around his eyes and that particular little hop of his jaw that told me he was doing his best to be understanding while lingering worry and doubt lived beneath the surface. Fair enough.

"I have one question," I said, knowing I was totally changing the subject and yet not, really. "About Jill?"

Crew did sigh this time, and when he looked down and away, the jaw hop turned to a jump, the twitch under his eye instantly registering as anger. But he did a great job of hiding it otherwise. If I hadn't made him furious myself a time or two (or six or, well, you know) in the past I might have missed it. "Jill's been... struggling with authority lately."

Huh. "What does that mean?"

Crew shrugged, eyes locked on mine, before taking a slow drink. He didn't speak, just stared at me like I should know what he meant while frustrated irritation almost made me poke him.

Leave it to my handsome sheriff boyfriend to change the subject. "I do like Noel Lewder for this, at least as a possible suspect." He reached for his notebook and flipped it open, frowning at his handwriting before going on. "Turns out she used to be a model, repped by Henry Ostler. She had some kind of breakdown last year during Fashion Week in New York. Henry dropped her and Grace fired her from her line. She started a blog bashing the industry and seems to blame Grace for some reason, not Henry, though it sounds like it was his decision to cancel their contract that ended her career."

"But why kill Faith Leeman?" Where was the motive to murder another model?

"Noel and Faith had several public fights when the blogger decided to go after some of Grace's favorite models directly." He closed his notebook and tucked it back into his pocket, still frowning slightly but from thought, not upset. "Noel's been bashing Grace and Faith, claiming that the designer's choice to use larger models, and I use that term loosely, is a sham, that Grace is as demanding of those who work for her as any other."

Hmmm. "But is that enough motive to kill Faith? We're obviously missing several pieces of the puzzle." We. Ahem.

Crew didn't correct me, though his eyes took on that sparkle of laughter that told me he caught the slip up and found it amusing. "No offense, but from what I've seen, many of the models I've met seem a bit high strung. And I've seen people kill for less."

True.

"As for Jill," Crew stood up, finishing his beer before his sentence, "let me handle it, okay? She's working some stuff out. She'll either shake this off or move on."

Shake what off? I didn't get to ask, the sound of the front door upstairs opening catching my attention. Fine, we'd talk about it later. And we would talk about it, make no mistake, Crew Turner.

When I reached the foyer, my boyfriend following close behind me, Petunia wriggling between my feet to make it to the newcomers faster than either of us, I found myself half-smiling, half-grimacing at Grace. The designer was in whispered conversation with Libby by the front door as if they'd entered together in the midst of what looked like a heated argument and came to an abrupt halt when their voices dropped below audible. It reminded me of seeing Libby with Henry earlier today, but I didn't mention it. Grace waved at me, offered her own sad smile, though, so I knew she wasn't unhappy to see me. She looked tired, worn thin, but still in control while Libby was a visible mess, her assistant shaking as she turned and saw me watching. The young woman hugged herself abruptly, falling instantly silent, almost sullen as she dropped her gaze to her feet while Petunia waddled to her side and sat next to her, panting her smiling pug smile up at the silent Libby.

The door opened before I could talk to Grace, Vivian slipping inside, instantly hugging her friend around her shoulders. If looks could put someone in the ground, the one Libby flashed at the Queen of Wheat would have buried Vivian so far beneath the earth she might have made it halfway to China. But was that jealousy or something else entirely?

"Grace." I ignored Libby and Vivian both, offering a hand which she took and held gently in hers. "I'm so sorry about Faith. Are you okay?"

The designer shook her head, dabbing at her nose with a tissue held in her other hand while Vivian stood there and supported her as if she'd fall over at any moment.

"I will be," Grace said, voice thick with grief. "It's all been such a shock."

"The show must go on, though, I assume." Crew sounded just a touch cynical, though he had his professional face on. "You'd like me to clear the crime scene so you can continue the show?"

Grace seemed shocked, paled out. "I don't know if I *can* go on," she whispered while Vivian glared at him.

"I'm sure some of the others might be so jaded," she snapped, "but Grace has a soul."

I waved her off, trying not to let my temper get the better of me. "Vivian." She scowled at me, gaze flashing to me instantly. "You're well aware Crew has been put in this position before. He's doing his best to anticipate. That's all."

Yikes. I didn't need to defend him. He was a grown man and sheriff. I hoped he wouldn't be offended. As for Vivian, she relented, sniffing softly before hugging Grace in a swift, protective motion.

"You had questions for Grace, Fee?" Vivian's eyes locked on mine. "Otherwise, I want to get her to bed."

Right, she was at the annex, not here at the main house. I hadn't expected to see her or Libby tonight. Vivian must have learned a thing or two watching me poke my nose in where it wasn't wanted. I glanced at

Crew who didn't comment. His expression seemed calm enough, whole body quiet and collected, not a hint of anger showing. So, I took the plunge and the initiative and nodded.

"Can you tell us what happened with Noel Lewder and why she held such animosity for you and Faith?" Way to just jump into heavy-duty questions, Fee. I should have asked Grace to the sitting room, let her take a load off, even gotten her some tea. Instead, I blurted out the big question at the top of my head and did my best not to wince when I finished.

Grace took it, well, gracefully. "I'd heard she's in town," she said, swallowing and stiffening a little as if trying to pull herself together. "She's been bitter over losing her contract with Henry and blames me for it, despite the fact I had nothing to do with it. Apparently, Faith told her I was the one who demanded he fire Noel. I did no such thing. I simply decided not to use her for my next show because she'd become so painfully thin."

"Against brand," Vivian said, like that needed to be made clear.

Grace nodded, touched her friend's hand. "Exactly. But Noel turned it into a vendetta against me and Faith and has been writing horrible things about us ever since. Not that it's altered my choice to continue to use more normal-sized models. If anything, her vitriol and near hysteria have proven to me that I'm on the right track. I want men and women who have bigger goals and dreams to represent my line. College students, professionals. People who take their lives seriously and treat modeling with reverence, not desperation."

"Sheriff Turner said she'd had a breakdown of some kind last year?" I glanced at him, surprised he was still seemingly content to remain silent.

Grace exhaled softly, face pinched with sorrow. "An unfortunate truth," she said. "In the middle of the runway, wearing Mateo Marney's latest masterpiece. She froze and then melted down. I was in the audience. It was... difficult."

"Disgusting, you mean." It was the first time Libby had spoken since Vivian's appearance and her tone held zero sympathy for Noel. "She freaked out like she was high or something and started tearing off the dress, threw pieces of it into the crowd while she screamed profanities at everyone. She even lunged at Henry, tried to attack him where he was sitting at the end of the runway." Libby didn't stop staring at the floor, but her frown spoke volumes of judgment. "They had to drag her away."

Grace didn't speak for a long moment after Libby finished but finally did before I could. "Noel claimed someone drugged her to make her snap like that. And I suppose it's possible. But she burned a lot of bridges that night and since then. It's a small community, really. Once you're labeled as difficult..." she spread both hands wide, the tissue in her right dangling between her thumb and index finger like a wounded butterfly. "She and Faith were never friends, not really. I wondered why Noel went after her so adamantly after the fact, though she didn't come out and accuse her of being the one who slipped her whatever made her crack."

Interesting. And definitely motive for murder, if that was the case.

Crew's barest nod told me he was thinking the same thing, his blue eyes turning to the staircase while I posed another question.

"Any idea why she'd be writing to Henry?" I saw Grace twitch, Libby's sudden guilty look, Vivian scowling. But it was Libby who answered.

"Isn't it obvious?" She snorted, finally looking up, so much anger behind her eyes I almost shivered. "She's been trying to get him to sign her again. Doing everything she can to get back on his good side." Was Libby doing the same for some reason? Did she realize speaking up made me wonder all the more what the two had been talking about?

"Someone should inform her that bashing the industry and those influential in it isn't helping her case." Vivian's crisp coldness was, at least, familiar, if not the comforting way she held Grace still.

"There's always the worry that Noel is trying to use Henry to ruin Grace." Libby didn't meet her boss's eyes, but some of the heavy fury was gone, at least. "Though I have no idea what she thought she had that could accomplish anything. Surely if she had information she thought relevant she would have posted it on that ridiculous blog of hers by now."

"Or not," Crew said, softly enough we all jumped just a bit, as if the women in the foyer had forgotten he was there. His tone stayed quiet as he went on like he dealt with nervous rabbits in a meadow, not three unhappy women (girlfriend excluded, of course). "If she had something that she could use against Grace and get her job back, it might be in her best interest to keep it from the public, bring it to Henry first."

That made sense to me.

"I have to ask." Crew cleared his throat, eyes locked on the designer. "Where were you earlier this evening, Ms. Fiore? Between 6:30 and 7PM?"

Grace's demeanor shifted from sorrowful to regret, though her dignified answer was precise and professional. "I was alone," she said, "working on new designs while I had dinner."

Crew didn't comment, just turned to Libby. "And you, Ms. Kim?"

Libby glanced at Grace, then Vivian, flinching slightly before she sighed and shrugged. I anticipated her answer but was just as surprised as the others when she responded with a name I wasn't expecting.

"I was with Mateo."

CHAPTER FIFTEEN

That admission got enough of a response from Grace and Vivian it was pretty clear Libby fraternizing with a rival designer wasn't exactly status quo. Made me wonder what they'd think about her cozy chat with Henry.

"I'm sorry," Libby gushed to her boss, regret clear, hand outstretched. "I was just talking to him. Not about work, I swear."

Grace's simple nod covered her initial reaction. "I understand," she said, turning away, toward the kitchen door and the pass through to the annex across the yard, before pausing to meet my eyes, hers sad all over again. "If there's nothing else, Fee?"

I glanced at Crew who didn't argue. "I'm sure a review of the tapes will prove you were where you said you were." Weak, but it gained me a smile from the designer.

"I'm sure." She nodded to Crew. "If you don't mind, Sheriff Turner, I'd like a chance to sleep a bit before I talk to you officially?"

Crew let her go without protest, Vivian glaring at him, then me, before leading Grace through the foyer and into the kitchen. He did stop Libby though, before the assistant could leave, with a gentle but insistent wave of his hand.

"I take it the nature of your visit with Mr. Marney was personal, then?" I caught myself blushing as Libby had her own slow, deep flush, before nodding. I just *bet* it was personal. "I'll confirm with him, of course."

Libby blanched then headed for the door. "Of course."

We watched her go, Petunia's yawn reminding me she was there as the oddly cat-like meow of it broke the tension of Libby's departure.

"Was anyone seen in the security footage entering the stage around the time of the murder?" I turned to Crew who continued to stare at the staircase as if contemplating the unfolding case without me. When he finally looked down and met my eyes, he shook his head.

"Alicia's working on it," he said. "Seems there was some kind of glitch. I'm going to check back with her in the morning."

Glitches weren't usually a coincidence, in my experience. Before I could comment as such, the door opened yet again, evening traffic always increased, I noticed, when someone was murdered, and Jill slipped through. She was dressed in uniform, at least, back in her deputy persona, but she didn't meet Crew's eyes and she seemed grim, angry, uncomfortable when she spoke.

"I finished the background checks," she said. Paused. "Sheriff."

Ugh.

"Thank you." Crew's tone held nothing of animosity though she sounded completely unhappy with him when she spoke again.

"I was going to text you," she said, enough anger in her voice I figured they'd had a conversation at some point I'd missed about communication, "but thought it would be best to deliver that in person." She finally met his eyes. "So, there's no confusion as to what I told you and what I didn't."

Whoops. Okay, this was going too far, especially when Crew's cool visibly cracked before he pulled himself together from the cheek tic and jaw leap in reaction to her words.

"A text would have been fine if I actually received it or an email or even a hint of what it is you were up to." They glared at each other while my gut clenched, and it became obvious to me what was going on.

Jill's side hustle. Had she forgotten to tell Crew and he gave her a hard time and now the two of them were acting like little kids over it? Sigh. But no, it had to be more than that.

My deputy friend shrugged and turned toward the

door. "Message delivered," she said. "And received. Sheriff." And then she was gone while I huffed at my boyfriend while he rubbed his forehead with one big hand like he knew I was about to give him a hard time.

"I'm pretty sure Jill's ready to quit." His voice was low, soft, sad. That cut off any kind of annoyed demands I might have placed on him to tell me details about their falling out. "She's been in a bad place for months, Fee. Since last August and Lester Patterson's murder."

It wasn't her fault Robert had been given the sheriff's seat when Crew disappeared to help out the FBI on a case he'd left unfinished. But yeah, come to think of it, she'd been acting weird, reserved. When I'd almost been killed in November when she'd failed to secure the firearms at the Black Mountain retreat, she'd been pretty hard on herself, and hard on me, too, come to think of it. Was she feeling like she had something to prove?

"I think she's being unduly influenced." Crew's hands settled at his hips, staring down at Petunia like she had answers to his most burning questions.

"Matt?" No, couldn't be. Her boyfriend was sweet, kind. And, if I was going to be honest, the park ranger wasn't the brightest bulb on the string.

Crew's lips thinned before he leaned forward and kissed my forehead. "You're usually faster on the uptake, Fleming."

And then it hit me. Like a ton of bricks and a runaway freight train and a cannonball to the solar plexus. "Robert." Snarl.

Crew didn't agree, didn't have to. Though, he did frown softly a moment later. "He's been putting a lot of pressure on her," he said. "But it's weird, Fee. Not like him, far too clever. Manipulative, you know? Twisted, smart pressure. Nothing of his usual heavy-handed idiocy."

Which told me the real culprit. "Has to be Rose." What did she have against Jill? Was Daisy's half-sister still trying to get her Robertkins into the sheriff's seat? Good luck, sister.

The sheriff's heavy sigh told me he'd come to the same conclusion. "No way he came up with this slow destruction of Jill's confidence on his own."

I touched his arm, hesitant and worried suddenly. They'd failed to take Crew down by force. Could they do it through slow and steady erosion? "You're okay?"

He laughed suddenly, hugged me, kissed my forehead, the delicious scent of him washing over me, shutting down my worry. "I've never been better, Fiona Fleming." He pushed me gently away and smiled down at me and for a long moment, it felt like he had something more to say.

Mom usually had amazing timing, but not so much tonight. She slipped through the kitchen door just as Crew's lips parted to speak.

"I'm sorry," she said, sounding contrite and genuinely apologetic, "but I need to see Fee."

Crew grinned at her, nodded, kissed me softly on the lips. "It can wait."

I let him go, watching that fine back end leave my foyer with enough heat in my cheeks I could have told my mother she had her own things to deal with and leave me out of it because I was following Crew home like the shameless, wonton hussy I was. Except, instead, I sighed out my desire and turned with reluctant obedience for the kitchen door and my mother's wicked grin.

"There'll be other evenings with the handsome sheriff," she whispered. "For now, we have a visitor. And you're going to want to hear what she has to say."

I followed Mom inside, realizing she probably didn't know Crew was on board with my investigation and had my back, protecting me, clear as glass when I laid eyes on Kami perched at the counter, the skinny young woman stuffing herself on fresh bread and butter like she had never eaten in her life.

CHAPTER SIXTEEN

Her guilt didn't stop her from shoving another dripping slice of carb-laden wheat goodness into her mouth, though I could tell from the way Kami's face twisted at the sight of me she struggled with her choice. I kept my expression as unjudging as possible and settled next to her, even smiling while she barely chewed, swallowed a giant mouthful and took another massive bite, this slice loaded down with a huge heap of Mom's strawberry jam dripping from the edges.

"Mom's the best cook, isn't she?" I helped myself to a piece, though with a bit more reserve when it came to the toppings. Kami took my participation as acceptance and beamed around the mouthful she fought to consume.

When she finally swallowed, she hugged herself, groaning softly. "This is the yummiest," she said, sing-songing the words. "Just the yummiest yummy I've ever had. Thank you, Lucy. You're the best."

Mom smiled at her, too, pushing the plate toward Kami who eyed the remaining three slices of fresh bread with a visible hunger that made me worry for the safety of the plate, Mom's fingers and anything else that came between the clearly starving young model and the heavenly scented slice of homemade goodness that begged for butter and jam. I'd cut back on the carbs myself lately, at least when I ate here at Petunia's, if only because Crew was so fond of pasta. But certainly, didn't make a huge deal about it and suddenly felt very sorry for the young woman who moaned her despair before diving for the last of the bread with zeal.

"I'm so sorry." She finally managed to talk around a bite a bit less gigantic, no longer a choking hazard, at least. "I'm not usually like this. It's just I fast when I'm about to do a show and I'm just so *hungry*."

No judging, Fee. No. Judging. "It can't be easy," I said instead.

She didn't need much prompting to keep talking, bobbing her head with great enthusiasm, her dark hair tied tight into a ponytail, the nondescript hoody and jeans she wore clear evidence she'd snuck her way in here. "It's awful," she said, eyes wide, unblinking as she licked at her fingers. "I'm going to pay for that." Regret came in a gush of guilt I could almost feel.

Great, all I needed was for her to crash and burn before she could fill me in on why she was here in the first place. Mom nodded quickly to me, and I leaped on the chance as Kami's hands settled on her flat stomach.

"I hear Grace is much more understanding about the size of her models." That seemed to be the right thing to say. Kami's face stilled, faint smile rising, and she appeared to pull herself out of the lure of her guilt long enough to answer.

"She's awesome," the young model said, sounding genuinely impressed. "She's different, you know? She cares about us. Don't get me wrong." She reached forward and grasped my wrist, her thin hand surprisingly strong. She was so tiny beside me, though taller than I was, reminding me of Willow though with more of a waifish look to her compared to my actor friend's ethereal beauty. "A lot of the designers are really wonderful, they're just... artists, you know? Distracted. Sometimes when they dress us it's like we're mannequins. Not people. But I'm not complaining." She wriggled on the stool, hands sliding into the front pouch of her dark blue hoody, far too big for her. "I have to keep reminding myself Grace sees me when we're working. And she's fine with me not being in perfect shape." Why did it sound like Kami didn't approve of that despite her clear love for all things carbs?

"Did you know Faith very well?" Maybe I could have been a bit more circumspect, but Kami seemed agreeable enough and she had to be here for a reason, right? Hopefully with information about the death. Why else would Mom have dragged me away from Crew the way she did? Besides, she'd been on my suspect list, what with the animosity the pair shared on the runway. Then again, I'd known Faith all of about a minute and couldn't stand her, so anyone could have been the murderer.

Fee. Be nice.

Kami's eye roll and exaggerated expression told me I'd supposed correctly. "Honestly, Faith was the worst." She sat back, looking between Mom and me like we should agree with her immediately. "You do this job long enough? You figure out what's what and who's in the know. And her list was the longest of anyone's."

Sounded helpful. "List?"

She chewed in ecstasy a moment before wiping at her lips with her fingertips, tucking crumbs into her mouth. "You know, a hit list. Stuff that we all play close. Details about people we can use to get ahead." She shrugged. "It's a thing."

Huh. "And you brought this to me why?"

Kami shrugged her thin shoulders inside the bulky sweater. "Vivian French brought me," she said. Ah, gotcha. "She said you'd be able to use what I've got better than the cops."

It wasn't like I had illusions about Vivian's faith in the Reading Sheriff's Department, but seriously. She was taking this whole Fee solve the murder thing to the limit. If Kami did have information about who killed Faith, it was just irresponsible to come to me first.

So, naturally, I did the obvious. "Go ahead," I said, contributing to the delinquency of the situation with willing participation and my own layer of guilt. "Tell me what you know."

Kami's grin lit her up and I realized as she spoke, she had no buried grief over the other model's loss. If anything, this was her true bread and butter, if you'll pardon the reference. "So, last year during Fashion Week, there was this big blow-up between Mateo and Faith. No one knew why." Her gossiping tone was about on point with the old ladies who watched every single thing that happened in the mean streets of Reading, and I had to suppress a giggle at the comparison. Focus, Fee. Murder investigation. "Anyway, that dress Faith was hung with?" How did Kami find out which dress it was? "She hated it. With a passion." Her breathless voice dropped in volume and timbre, and I found myself leaning close, Mom, too, to catch every word. "She went all diva about it, since it was a co-create with Mateo but Grace insisted she wear it." Kami's disdain for Faith's unhappiness made her look like a thirteen-year-old girl in a high school spat. "She should have known not to argue. We don't argue with designers. We wear their clothes." Her hands exited the pouch and cut through the air in front of her like two quick karate chops. "End of story." Skin slapped denim as her arms dropped. "Faith had attitude." She glanced behind her though we were alone as if checking to be sure no one overheard. Petunia's soft whine of protest she'd been forgotten in the bread feast frenzy was the only sound before Kami went on, voice low again. "She complained. A lot. And not just about the clothes. About the other models. She called them *fat*." Kami seemed shocked by that, though I wasn't sure if she was surprised Faith used the word or what. "She didn't want to comply with Grace's sizing rules. They had a fight about her being underweight just yesterday."

Okay, so two more suspects, one of them the person Vivian wanted me to exonerate. And honest, I was rather a fan of Grace's myself, so if I could find evidence Mateo did do it, all the better.

Right, because I was in the business of cheering for possible murderers. Now, who was judging?

"Does it bother you, following Grace's rules?" Mom spoke up, startling Kami who shrugged, though her guilty expression returned.

"It's great," she said, "Except. Well, when we're working for Grace, she wants us a certain size. But when we go to work for the other designers or check in with our agents..." She looked suddenly uncomfortable all over again. "It's been a bit of a struggle." She burped softly, rubbing her stomach. Then, she brightened, leaning into me again. "Oh, and Mateo!" She winked, a naughty look crossing her face. "He's been sleeping with Libby, or at least he was a month ago. I caught them at it."

Interesting, considering Libby worked for Grace. Was someone trying to frame the designer? Henry and Mateo working together, perhaps?

"Is that relevant to the case?" I realized at that moment Kami might not have had justice for Faith in the forefront. Her nose wrinkle of wicked delight told me I was right.

"Probably not," she giggled, "but I have tons more gossip if you have more of that delicious bread to share."

CHAPTER SEVENTEEN

Mom took Kami in hand after that, summoning Dad to drive the young model home while I did some online digging. The fact my P.I. father wasn't interested in lingering, didn't suggest Mom do the driving honors to stay with me and butt his nose into said internet research, told me he thought he already had the clues he could glean and was likely going to take the time during the drive to pick Kami's little brain clean.

Let him. I had my own ideas. Okay, so that might make it sound as if there was a competition or something going on between me and my dad. Who could solve the case faster or an equally ridiculous supposition that had nothing to do with the truth. Right? We were supposed to be partners—at least, he'd thrown me into the ring without my knowledge or approval—so any kind of withholding of evidence from each other wasn't in either of our best interests.

Except, of course, this was my dad we were talking about, and I was my father's daughter.

Snort.

Noel Lewder's blog was easy enough to find, the disgruntled and bitter model's rambling diatribe against the fashion industry with enough truth nuggets to hold up but layered all over with the level of nasty resentment and whiny poor me that made my teeth ache like I'd eaten too much chocolate. From Henry to Mateo to Frederick, Noel had horrible things to say—accusing the last of assault and pressuring her into inappropriate acts. Since I had first-hand experience with Frederick Newmark's particular brand of yuck, I was inclined to side with Noel on that one and struggled, then, not to judge everyone she wrote about.

Except when it came to Grace. Everything I read about her from the ex-model's perspective made Noel sound like her complaints were sour grapes, though there were enough supportive comments at the end of each post I figured Noel was being fed by those who would have preferred Grace wasn't as popular as she was.

A quick check on Faith turned up a large array of photo spreads, advertising campaigns and her own personal website. Every post I came across, including old social media shares, all pointed to Faith being well-loved and admired. Which instantly put my back up and got my suspicions stirring. No one that willful and, according to Kami, confrontational, was universally loved. Certainly not as flawless as her online persona would have led me to believe.

As for Henry Ostler, his modeling agency had enough big names on the roster he was clearly on the up-and-up, not one of those scammer companies that took advantage of the young men and women they contracted. Though, for all I knew, every agency was a scam. I did catch a sniff of an old newspaper article, from New York a few years ago, suggesting he was being investigated for further accusations of a sexual nature connected to a model that turned out to be a minor. But, as I read further, I realized it wasn't Henry who was the actual accused, but Frederick Newmark.

Personal experience tied to a trend, even if unsubstantiated? Enough for me to play judge and jury. Interesting. Frederick worked for Henry at one time, wasn't just repped by him as a designer, and had embroiled his boss in his troubles. How lovely of him, though the pair seemed to have worked out the issue because there was no later story and nothing I could find in the court system that suggested he even pled out. And Frederick's name was listed as part of Henry's current agented roster.

I took a quick swipe at Libby, realizing almost immediately the girl was an enigma. No social media, no blog, no real anything. All I could find was her bio pic on Grace's website, and it didn't even really look like her. Felt instantly sketchy and I made a note to ask Grace about her assistant's past, especially since it seemed the girl had only been working for her for six months or so if the bio was correct. And yes, I would share with Crew. But not Dad. He could uncover her lack of background himself.

Competitive, who, me?

Mateo Marney, on the other hand, was all over the internet, from one scandal to another, always involving gorgeous young women, and sometimes even those who were married and should have been off his radar. At least he seemed to love his flamboyant life. There were a few images of him with Faith, one of the two of them fighting backstage at Fashion Week, confirming Kami's gossip. So, he was definitely on the list of suspects, if only because the idea of giving a smarmy guy a hard time appealed to me.

Oh, Fee.

Frederick's headshots made me cringe. Why he thought biting the arm of his thick, black glasses and trying to look coy appealed was beyond me. More ew than I could shake a stick at, even if he hadn't hit on me. Again, I uncovered a few hints of him being inappropriate, but nothing concrete and certainly nothing that ended up in the courts or the papers as an actual full-blown scandal. Did he have something against Faith? Or did she have something against him?

I purposely left Grace for last, squirming uncomfortably as I finally sighed and searched her name. Thing was, almost everything I uncovered reconfirmed to me she was genuine and the kind of person I really wanted to get to know better. Mind you, I had to admit I'd been fooled in the past. I'd fallen under the friendship spell—and once, more than friendship—of those who turned out to be guilty. But I just couldn't bring myself to doubt the charming and forthright designer so, when all I uncovered on the negative were those who complained about her use of larger than wafer-thin models, I abandoned my query.

And hesitated, thought it over. Typed Vivian's name into the search bar. Before deliberately backspacing until the box stood empty, cursor blinking, waiting for input. She'd given up modeling, abandoned her past for her family's business. Yes, I was curious about her, about her career and honestly wanted to know if she was as good at modeling as she was being the Queen of Wheat. Why then did it feel like an invasion of her privacy to go looking? After all, the internet was a public space. Anything on there was fair game. Wasn't it?

I shut down the computer and sat back, frowning at the closed laptop on my coffee table, Petunia snoring softly next to me while I admitted Dad might beat me to the truth this time. I had almost nothing to go on, certainly no evidence of murderous intent. And I could have been at Crew's all this time.

Sighing, frustrated, wondering why I even cared Vivian asked me to be a busybody, I went to bed.

I slept better than I expected and woke with a new direction of inquiry. A quick hug for Daisy and

Mom after my morning rounds and I took a stroll to the center of town, to French's Handmade Bakery, in search of the Queen herself. If she wanted me to solve this murder, she could dig deep and tell me everything she knew. Which meant maybe, just maybe, I might get permission to find out who she really was.

CHAPTER EIGHTEEN

It didn't take long for me to find out Vivian wasn't at work, and I contemplated just going back to Petunia's when her manager, Margaret Peadly, informed me of that fact. Except that she then filled in the rest of the information, prompting a fresh inspiration. "Vivian is home today," Margaret said. "She always takes Monday off."

Huh. Good to know, though why Vivian would take such a random day to herself I had no idea but was suddenly eager to find out. Margaret's instant flicker of what looked like regret at telling me so was all the more fodder for my imagination and I left French's with a single goal in mind.

Thing was, I'd never actually been to Vivian's house before, though I knew where she lived, naturally. Her big, white home with the stunning wrought iron fence and massive gate build into towering brick cornerstones was a fixture in Reading. I'd walked and biked past here many times as a child and teenager, though I hadn't had much reason to come to this part of town since I came home from New York. Even deeper in the rich part of town, neck-high with all the residences of the people who only came to Reading a few weeks a year, their vacation houses locked up tight and a bone of contention with local residents, Vivian's was one of the only mansions—yeah, I called it a mansion—that had year-round living.

I paused at the gate, my little car humming softly as I contemplated the call panel. There was a good chance Vivian would reject a visit from me. Then again, she'd asked me to look into this murder for her, so maybe she'd let our lifelong mutual animosity slide the rest of the way to the ground in favor of information that might help her friend. When I leaned out my window and pressed the button, a woman's voice answered instantly.

"Can I help you, Ms. Fleming?"

Did I know her? She clearly knew me. "I'm here to talk to Vivian." I let it go at that. Yes, I could have played the Grace card and I was, after all, here to talk to the Queen of Wheat about the case. But it felt heavy-handed to mention the designer Vivian seemed so deeply connected to.

"Of course. Please, come right up." I heard the mechanism of the gate click as it swung slowly, ponderously, inward. "You can park by the front door."

Why was I suddenly nervous? I hit the gas, cruising up the drive to the large, open entry to the house, parking as discretely as I could near the wide front steps to the looming front door, knowing I looked like the country mouse coming to visit her city mouse cousin, wishing I'd at least taken a moment to neaten my typically messy ponytail that used to be an effort at a bun at the nape of my neck, refusing to look down at the front of my t-shirt to check for stains. Purposely straightening my shoulders and choosing confidence over the rush of inadequacy I was feeling, I took the steps two at a time, the short flight barely giving me time to reach the landing before the front door swept open and an older woman smiled from the interior.

Hey, I did know her, didn't I? I smiled back, tentative, until she held out one hand and ushered me toward her, her own expression shifting from welcome to beaming.

"So lovely to see you again, Ms. Fleming." She had the faintest British accent as if she'd been born in England but spent most of her life here in the States. I shook her hand when she grasped for mine, mind whirling as I tried to place her. "You probably don't remember me." Whoops, was it that obvious? "I haven't seen you since you were a little girl and you and Miss Vivian were friends and playmates." Huh, what? Since when? All I remembered of our past was Vivian bullying Daisy and me breaking her nose with a solid punch. That was the definitive memory moment I had for the Queen of Wheat. Since when had we been friends?

"Nice to see you again," I said. And hesitated.

"Clara French, Miss Fleming," she said with that same smile. She was older than Mom by at least a decade, her hair untouched by artificial color, a solid and dependable steel gray cut short enough to be no-nonsense. Her blue eyes matched Vivian's and I had to wonder how they were related, the much more practical Clara seemingly comfortable in her fuzzy cardigan, cream blouse, past-the-knee twill skirt and comfortable shoes. "I'm Vivian's auntie. Her dear departed Uncle Stanley was my husband."

Ah, so they were related by marriage. I felt myself relax in her presence as she turned and gestured for me to move past the doorway and into the main foyer. I loved the newly renovated entry to the annex, but this place put Jared and Alicia's efforts to shame. I'd known Vivian was wealthy, sure. But her vaulted ceilinged, winding wooden-staircased, marble-floored extravaganza made me feel even more like a commoner come calling on royalty.

Queen of Wheat indeed.

I followed Clara into the house, to the left and through a towering doorway arched in heavy crown molding that made me feel tiny in comparison, the quiet and faintly rose-fragranced air of the place giving me goosebumps. I found myself in a large sitting room, a circle of antique wing-backed chairs in the center, a huge fireplace with a white marble mantle looking big enough to fit a whole tree inside. My sneakers whispered over the lush carpeting, the looming oppression of the volume of the place cutting off my usual flippancy and honestly making me feel like I'd made a huge mistake coming here.

And yet, this house seemed familiar after all, and as I ventured further, Clara leading me toward the chairs in the middle of the room, huge windows letting in light from the front of the house, I realized she was right. I'd been here before. How had I not remembered knowing Vivian as a child? Maybe because I hadn't wanted to?

"Martha, sweetness, we have a visitor." Clara smiled at me again, gesturing for me to join her and, to my surprise, a tiny older woman nestled deep into one of the wingbacks like she lived in it. A twinge of something hit me as I sank down next to her, frowning and reaching for her hand as Martha reached back, thin fingers lined with veins, but surprisingly strong for her apparent frailty.

"Lucy, darling," she said in a clear, high voice, "how lovely of you to come visit us."

Clara winced a bit, her smile turning sad as she leaned in and patted Martha's hand. "My mother-in-law has difficulty with the passage of time," she said. "She knew your mother well, Miss Fleming."

"Fiona, please." I held Martha's hand while she clung to me, leaning toward me, her tiny face scrunched with wrinkles but her blue eyes sparkling in delight.

"Lucy, sweet girl, you bring that handsome

deputy boyfriend of yours over sometime." She giggled like a teenager, lips twitching. "I want to pinch that fine bottom again."

I laughed, unable to stop myself, the idea that this old lady had a thing for my dad making me equally nervous and amused. "I'll do that," I said, winking at Clara. "I'm sure he'd love it."

Martha laughed, sinking back into her seat, the fur blanket tucked around her falling away from the simple cream dress she wore. Clara instantly tucked her back in before perching on the armrest of the wingback, both of them smiling at me like they expected something from me.

I cleared my throat, not sure what to say, and got to business. "I'm here to ask Vivian some questions about her friend, Grace Fiore."

Clara clucked softly, Martha's face tightening in a frown a moment as she seemed lost in confusion. Dementia, had to be. From what I understood of the illness, though, she'd reached a ripe old age and still appeared to be bright enough. I'd be so lucky.

"Sad business," Clara said, patting Martha's hand that she held between her own, resting in her lap. These two ladies obviously spent a great deal of time together, the elder looking to the younger for what seemed like direction, with adoration on her face, and I wondered then how long they'd spent here, in this house, alone or at least isolated from the rest of the world. Sad on the one hand, and yet, again, I'd be so lucky to have someone to spend my life with who loved me as much as these two obviously did. "Poor

Viv dear is in a state over the whole thing."

I coughed softly, shocked to find I was choked up and needing to redirect my attention, so I didn't start crying for no reason. Right, Fee. No reason at all. "I understand. That's why I'm here. I need to get some information straight."

Martha tugged on my hand, pulling me closer, the little bow of her mouth puckering as she whispered. Well, tried to whisper, likely thought she was, that faint scent of roses rising from her clothing as she drew near. I focused on her still-bright eyes, the pure white curls of her hair falling around her in a delicate veil, and I knew I was looking at Vivian's future.

"Iris, darling," she said, surprising me again. She'd forgotten she'd called me by my mother's name already, instead labeling me as my departed grandmother. I didn't get to recover from that shock because she went on. "Why doesn't Marie come around anymore? I miss her so."

"Marie Patterson?" Wow. I glanced at Clara whose face pinched a moment, again in sorrow.

She shrugged, stared at the tiny hand clutched between her two. "Iris and Marie used to be dear friends. Martha was the oldest, but they, along with a few others," Peggy Munroe for one, Doreen Douglas another that I knew of, "had a bit of a ladies club back in the day."

Ladies club, huh? "I'm sorry," I said to Martha, squeezing her hand. "I'm sure she'll come to visit soon." Weak, Fee. A sad attempt to comfort an old lady. But it worked. Martha perked instantly, her cheeks turning pink as she pulled me tightly to her and kissed me on the corner of my mouth.

"Sweet girl," she whispered, really whispered this time. "Do you still have the doubloon? We'll need it if Marie's guess was right. And I'm sure she's right. Reading's treasure will be ours, just like we planned."

And, in that instant, the entire world went away. Murder, mayhem, Vivian, Grace, all of it. Every last scrap of anything that troubled me lately went out the proverbial window as I gaped and gasped for breath while Martha released my hand long enough to pinch my cheek and giggle.

So. Many. Questions. Here then could be the source of answers for the Reading hoard. Right in front of me, practically in my lap—or me in hers—and all I had to do was ask.

"Fiona." Vivian's cold voice cut through the moment, jerking me out of the tunnel-vision tension I felt and sending Martha back into her chair, where she picked at her blanket and hummed softly to herself.

I stood, trembling, knowing I had to look pale, shaken, but Vivian was equally so and I found myself staring at her as she visibly pulled herself together, gesturing for me to follow her.

Clara stood as well, face pinched and unhappy. "Viv, dear—"

"Mind your own business, Auntie." Vivian's snapped response had an instant effect on Clara who nodded and sat down again, abruptly, hand clasping for Martha. As for the old woman, she was utterly lost now in whatever world she usually inhabited, ignoring me while I struggled to come up with an excuse to talk to her further.

Instead, frustrated and bubbling with fresh anxiety over being so close to answers to a riddle that had plagued me since my return to Reading, I joined Vivian who practically herded me out into the foyer away from the two quiet ladies I couldn't feel anything but sorry for.

"Ta ta for now, Iris, darling," Martha called after me. "Secrets best kept, my love."

CHAPTER NINETEEN

Vivian's expression was about as cold as was to be expected, though I couldn't get past her initial reaction and how she'd seemed so vulnerable, trembling as I'd been trembling, though I imagined for different reasons.

What was she hiding? The two sweet ladies in the other room were nothing to be ashamed of, were they? At least she seemed to be taking care of them, I'd give her that. But the impression I had they were somehow trapped here, like prisoners in this gilded cage of wealth and old secrets gave me the shivers like nothing else, not even murder. What did Vivian have to do with Marie Patterson and, more importantly, did she have a key to the treasure?

"You're not welcome here." Vivian didn't stop at

the foyer, escorting me all the way to the front door and out onto the step where she firmly shut the big entry behind her. She even went so far as to cross her thin arms across her chest and glare at me like I'd somehow broken some code of conduct we'd agreed to even though we'd done nothing of the sort. I wanted to ask her if she remembered we were friends when we were little, but that annoyingly icy stare of hers just set me off like always.

Nice to know no matter what happened Vivian French and her better than everyone else attitude was a constant.

"I had questions," I said. "You wanted me to investigate, right? That was the gist of your demands on me when you brought this mess into my life?"

Vivian flinched but didn't relent. "Alicia did first," she said, voice soft, defensive.

Grunt. "Listen," I said, temper heating my words more than they would have any other time, if only because I still reeled from the reveal of the possibility her grandmother had information I needed to solve the hoard mystery and I now had zero access to her, "I'm here because you asked me to be. If you decide you want to leave things to Jill and Crew and Robert, you just say the word, Viv." I watched her face fall, her clenched body unwind slightly, my own flare of anger retreating as she nodded, arms dropping to her sides.

"I just wasn't expecting…" She glanced behind her, caught herself, tried for rigid control again but didn't quite make it. It gave me a brief and sad insight into Vivian I hadn't had before. She wasn't angry I intruded. She was terrified of what I'd seen, protective of the women she guarded within. Did she think she was doing them a favor, keeping them safe from the outside world? Or was she truly hiding something? In a flash I remembered Vivian had lost her twin brother when they were little, the truth hitting me almost like a blow. Wait, I remembered him, Victor. He'd drowned, hadn't he?

Vivian's expression finally settled, and I knew any chance of asking her questions was gone with her return to control. "I'm sorry." Wow, an apology? Blunt and abrupt, but one nonetheless. Okay then. I nodded as she went on. "What do you need from me that brought you here and couldn't wait until I was available?"

So much for saying she was sorry. That was as backhanded a complaint as ever I heard one. Still, I let her have her victory if only because I now had her voice in my head apologizing for the times I needed to call up something to keep me warm at night. Oh, Fee. So cynical.

I ran through my questions quickly enough, recapping what I'd learned online and gained little new from her. Though, when I reached the topic of Frederick and the accusations against him, Vivian actually flinched, if barely perceptible. Thing was, I was so in tune with her at this point I almost twitched with her and caught myself before I impulsively reached out to take her hand in comfort.

Weird. Get it together, Fleming.

147

Meanwhile, Vivian's chin came up, lips twisting in a wry show of distaste. "Frederick has a certain reputation," she said. "I myself had to fend him off when I modeled for Henry." She looked sad in that moment. Like her past was something she wished she could abandon at the side of the road and never have to think about again. "I'm certain he's never changed, but he's harmless, in his own way. At least to those as experienced as Faith Leeman."

"That's horrible." My stomach turned over, empathy for Vivian, for all the young men and women who worked in the industry she still seemed to pine over as if the loss of a loved one. How could she idolize working in an environment like that?

Vivian shrugged, delicate but powerful, icy eyes unflinching. "It's part of the culture," she said. "Modeling is all about being seen as an object, Fiona. Surely that much is obvious." It was, but it didn't make it right. "That's why I'm so in support of Grace and her vision." As always, Vivian's voice changed when she spoke about her designer friend, warming up, softening. "She doesn't just love fashion. She loves the people in it and wants to do her part to improve the industry. To make it not just a beautiful vision on the outside, but the same on the inside."

I wasn't going to argue with Vivian about her optimism. She seemed to have so little of her own and telling her that my own jaded opinion of the fashion industry that tried every day through photoshopped images to make me feel fat, ugly and unworthy was likely going to remain the status quo.

Instead, I asked my final question. "All the information I have on Faith says she was well-loved, pretty squeaky clean. Does that sound accurate?"

Vivian's instant irritation told me it didn't. "I can assure you, anyone who made it to the level Faith had didn't do so on looks alone." She glanced over her shoulder at the door, anxiety a whisper across her face before returning her attention to me for one last moment. "Find out what she had on those around her, and you might find the murderer."

Nice of her to tell me this earlier. "Blackmail?"

"More than likely just leverage." Vivian turned her back on me, grasped the doorknob. Hesitated. "Fee." She cleared her throat, glancing back over one shoulder, not quite meeting my eyes. "Please, ignore anything you heard from Auntie and Grandam. They are both very old and tend to ramble." She paused one last moment. "And the next time you want to speak with me, call. I'll come to you."

I didn't get to comment. With that, she pulled the door open just wide enough to slip through, closing it behind her with a thump of finality. If Vivian thought I was going to listen to her, she had another thing coming. Because not only did she give me confirmation I absolutely needed to pay attention to what they'd said, dementia driven or not, her nervousness was more than enough impetus for me to believe what I already suspected was true.

Vivian French was deep in the Patterson camp and couldn't be trusted.

CHAPTER TWENTY

I drove home, musing the entire way, wondering how Crew and I could manage to get into the marina and dive for the evidence I'd seen last August, a chance to investigate the compass I knew was carved into the stone under the main pier at the yacht club. We'd both tried a couple of times to find a good excuse to do so, but neither of us could come up with a valid reason. I hadn't given the hoard much thought in the last little while, my mind more taken up by Siobhan Doyle, by Daisy and Rosebert, by Crew (okay, so mostly by Crew, so sue me) and the busy life that Petunia's and the annex tied me to. Like always, for some reason, new shiny took me over, older mysteries falling to the wayside. Maybe partially because I worried Rose knew more than I wanted her to? The thought she and Robert might uncover evidence thanks to me being clumsy about my own investigation made me queasy. Besides, the hoard had waited this long, hadn't it? I hadn't had the impetus to leap on the question in the last little while

But now? Now that I had the secretive questioning of an old woman to refuel the fire of my curiosity? I'd be talking to my fellow conspirators and taking some definitive steps.

In the meantime, I had some research to dig up. Namely on Vivian's family, on her deceased twin brother and the ties she had to the Patterson family, if any.

Mom and Daisy were in the kitchen when I arrived home and I immediately told them about meeting the ladies. I left out Martha's little hint about the treasure, but the rest of it was met with sadness and quiet, at least on Mom's part. Daisy even appeared troubled by what I told them, and that was saying something since she wasn't really a Vivian fan and never had been.

"It's true," Mom said, voice soft and low while she poured me a cup of coffee, adding extra cream as if doing so might give me comfort. Like the plate of coffee cake she shoved at me and I realized in a start of wonder my mother didn't just love to cook, she used food as love itself. I nibbled the cake as she went on. "Iris used to take us to the French's for Sunday tea. That's how you met Vivian, so many years ago, Fee. You were friends until you started school and her mother's influence kicked in." Mom blinked, sniffed softly. "Poor Victor. You were there, you know. The day he drowned. You saved Vivian, Fee, but Victor died."

I *what?* "Why don't I remember any of this?" Did I block it out? I reached for memories, didn't find any, while Mom nodded.

"You were traumatized. Victor was even closer to you than Vivian. John and I never mentioned it because the psychologist who examined you after the fact said you'd forgotten everything. On purpose, I suppose, to protect yourself. And, with time, we forgot, too. Though, I think we never really did."

I chewed at my bottom lip, heart pounding. "Is that why Vivian doesn't like me?"

Mom shook her head, patted my hand. "Poor Vivian doesn't like herself, dear," she said, sounding like that was the most tragic truth that there ever was, and I had to agree with her. Sure, I beat myself up from time to time, but I actually thought I was pretty awesome. Vivian had it all, but to not like herself, well. How long could someone live like that and not be miserable? "I blame her mother, that horrible creature."

Daisy nodded, leaned in, sighed. "I've never gotten along with Vivian, Fee, you know that. But Lucy's right. Her mother was a monster. You think Vivian's cold?"

I couldn't recall Mrs. French at all. "What happened? Vivian was modeling, wasn't she?" I missed all of that, leaving for college right after high school the way I had. I still didn't like thinking about that time in my life, the way I'd gone, how I'd hurt myself and my parents. Better to focus on Vivian's troubles than my old news, right? "Why did she come back?"

"Her father." Mom patted my hand. "He passed in a tragic accident when Vivian was twenty-one. Her mother knew nothing about the business, was going to ruin them."

"I hear she lives in Boston now." Daisy stole a corner of coffee cake, huge gray eyes full of compassion I wasn't sure she'd ever actually let Vivian see.

Mom snorted, her least favorite reaction since it was so unladylike but one she pulled out when she was feeling particularly irritated. "A dilettante, living off her daughter and old family money. Rachelle doesn't have anything to do with Vivian these days, as far as I know. And the better for it." Wow, I had no idea my mother felt that protective of the woman I'd spent most of my life despising and judging. Mom relented, eating her own bite of sugary goodness before going on. "Vivian learned quickly, came home and took over, just like that." She snapped her fingers.

Daisy flipped open the laptop she'd set on the counter and, after a short search, showed me some images of a familiar and yet stunningly unfamiliar young woman featured in several advertising campaigns. Okay, Vivian was gorgeous. I got the picture, literally.

"Martha and Clara?" I prodded Mom with those

two names.

"Dear old Martha," Mom said. "She and Iris were close, once upon a time. I think she's suffering from dementia." I nodded as my mother shook her head in sorrow. "A shame. She had a sharp mind and always made me laugh. As for Clara, she's a dear, married Vivian's uncle and immigrated from England years ago."

For a moment I had a thought. Could she be somehow connected to Siobhan? And then I gave myself a headshake. Two different countries, England and Ireland. Besides, I was reaching for straws in that connection, right?

Wasn't I?

"Mom," I said, chasing back that murmur of curiosity in favor of answers to questions right in front of me (because who didn't need unexamined details floating to the surface of their mind at three in the morning?), "what connection does Vivian have to the Pattersons? I know Grandmother Iris was friends with Marie. And it seems that Martha was, too. Do you think Vivian is still tied to them?"

Mom didn't answer right away, but her troubled look gave me pause. "All I know, dear, is that when Vivian came home after her father's death, French's was in a terrible state. And shortly thereafter Vivian had everything back up and running properly, was in firm control, though she was barely out of her teens and had no experience with business."

Meaning it was possible the Pattersons stepped in to help out and now they owned her soul. So be it.

On the other hand, I couldn't help the grudging admiration I felt for her. She'd not only given up her dream, she'd done what she had to in order to support her family, to save her father's business. I didn't want to admire her, not right now, but it was hard not to.

Damn it.

My phone buzzed, catching my attention and I did a quick check while Mom and Daisy went their separate ways, the sound of the front doorbell calling my bestie while my mother returned to her endless cooking routine.

Sorry to cancel short notice. Crew's text disappointed, but it wasn't his fault. *Something came up. Work.*

I understand. The least I could do was not let him know I was shallow enough to feel annoyed at the fact I wasn't going to see him tonight. *Stay safe and if you need me, I'm here.*

Love you.

Okay, he was totally forgiven. *Love you, too.*

I retreated a moment to my apartment, Petunia ignoring me in favor of sitting at Mom's feet as she always did while my mother was cooking and did my own quick search of Vivian at last. On impulse, I picked up the phone and dialed the *Reading Reader Gazette*.

"I'm not here," Pamela's gruff voice said. "I have better things to do than sit in the office. Leave a message and if it's important, I'll get back to you. Eventually." I grinned at the familiar message, waiting for the beep.

"It's Fiona," I said. "You better call me." And hung up. Pamela might not be willing to talk, her lean toward her wife's family and toeing the company line lately worrying at best. Still, if I could get her in a chatty mood, I might be able to figure out what the Pattersons had on Vivian and, indirectly, get a line on what the ladies club knew about the treasure.

So many threads hanging around me, I felt like I was being tickled on all sides. Only one was a real priority, though, wasn't it? With a deep sigh, I headed back upstairs, determined to help Vivian find out who killed Faith Leeman.

And while our initial interaction had left me with a bad taste in my mouth, not to mention the implied—if not court proved—behavior of the older designer was about as cringe-worthy as anyone could ask for, I had questions for Frederick Newmark and, darn it, I was going to ask them.

I ran through what I wanted to ask on my drive to the lodge, but all of that went out the window when I actually set foot in the place, uncommon discomfort making me squeamish. He had to be in his room, didn't he? I knocked, did my best to be polite and professional but knew immediately I'd made an error when his smile turned predatory, and he gestured for me to enter.

Yeah, not happening. "I'm fine in the hall," I said, firm enough he would surely get the hint. Apparently not. He leaned into the door frame like it was sexy, jutting his hips toward me with a kind of practiced sneer/smile meant to seem sensual, I think. More yuck. Awesome.

"What can I do for you, beautiful?" He up and downed me. Like, out and out looked me over from head to toe. He was a cheek slap waiting to happen.

I kept a solid three feet between us and launched into my questions. "How well did you know Faith Leeman?" Smarm made my skin creep and I just wanted this to be over.

His vapid gaze snapped into irritation. "I thought you were here to talk to me."

"I am." Seriously, what was his definition of talking?

Frederick eye-rolled, flicking his fingers at me, gold ring flashing in the light. "She was a model." He sounded disinterested, glancing down at his hand and gasping softly, holding his fingertips up to the light. "I'm in desperate need of a mani-pedi. But this place is booked."

Dear god, the man was clueless. "What about Kami Derham?"

His gaze flickered to me, another frown appearing. "Model." He waited like he'd told me everything he knew.

This was a total waste of time. "And where were you last night at 6:30PM?"

He tilted his head to one side, frowning over my shoulder before shrugging. "I don't keep track of every minute. Maybe eating?" He pursed his lips. "No, I'm fasting today. Wait, you said today? Is it that late already?"

Argh. "Thanks," I said. "Never mind."

His silky smile of grossness returned while he gestured to his open door. "Care for a drink?"

I desperately needed one. And a shower. Instead, I tossed my hands and left, grumbling to myself about why I even bothered.

CHAPTER TWENTY-ONE

I almost immediately ran into Jill when I veered off toward the ballroom, and not just metaphorically. She was heading one way and I the other, sneaking (yes, I admit I was sneaking) into the staging area set up in the ballroom while she was doing what I could only guess were her rounds. Our matching squeaks of surprise made me giggle, and, for a moment, she matched my humor, though hers quickly faded when she settled into a more judging persona.

"I can't let you in here, Fee." Since when? I didn't like the frown now pulling at her lips or the scowl making her eyes look small under heavy brows, the bully expression nothing like the woman I'd befriended over the last few years. The Jill I'd come to know and admire was open-minded, smart as a whip and ready to do what it took to solve a crime. I felt instead like I was staring into the face of a brick wall, immovable and inflexible under that dark suit she wore.

"Vivian asked me to help." I knew that wasn't a good reason to be backstage, though since Vivian was one of the sponsors... never mind this was a crime scene at the moment and not a fashion show anymore. Sophistry.

Jill's expression softened nonetheless, and I wondered at her shift in attitude. "I'm sorry, I can't." She seemed suddenly torn and I had to admit she must have been between a rock and a very hard place.

"Tough being a deputy and the hired help for the show," I said, going for commiseration instead of aggression. After all, Jill was my friend. Heck, I'd been the one to encourage Matt to finally ask her out. We'd been through numerous murder investigations together and she'd always had my back and me hers. I hated feeling like we were at odds all of a sudden. Especially when she clearly thought she needed to express her friendship for me before this particular mess turned into one.

Jill hesitated, arms falling to her sides, face twisting from scowl to anxiety and I realized I'd hit the nail directly on the head. "I don't know what to do, Fee," she whispered, leaning toward me, glancing right and left as if we'd be overheard. "I never expected this to happen. It was supposed to be an easy gig, a bit of extra money. Not a full-blown murder investigation and I'm on the other side."

"You don't have to be." I reached out and squeezed her arm, then let her go when she flinched and pulled away. "Jill, you work for Reading, not Grace or Henry. Crew needs you."

That didn't go over well, her face shifting once more to a scowl. "So you say," she snapped, leaning away again. "Don't even try it, Fee. I'll put you in cuffs and toss you in a cell if you try to break in."

Wow, where did my friend go? "You can talk to me," I said, hoping she could hear the distress in my voice, see it on my face. I did nothing to try to hide it and though it might have been a ploy with anyone else, this was Jill. I wasn't faking.

She uncoiled yet again, this time her anxiety so deep it seemed painful. "I'm sorry," she said. "Fee, I'm just doing my job. Please don't make me choose between my friendship and my duty."

But which duty was she upholding? Because Crew had already given me permission to dig, right? I almost commented, thought about arguing, debated internally, then sighed and tossed my hands.

"Whatever," I said. "You think I want to be here?" She shrugged, looked away. "Honestly, I've had my fill of dead bodies, thanks." That got a bit of a smile, faint but there. "Nightmares for years." She was one of the only people I'd told about my recurring panicked dreams filled with hanging next to corpses while swinging from trees and being crushed under the weight of moaning zombies and drowning as I sank under dark water. I knew she understood and the compassionate flash of emotion that touched her eyes told me she still considered me a friend. "I'm tired of death," I said. "And I wouldn't be here if Vivian hadn't asked me." Come to think of it, why *was* I here? I hesitated myself, feeling my shoulders slump. "The last thing I want is to damage our friendship over this, Jill." I let that sink in before adding the second load of guilt. "Or to make things worse between you and Crew."

I know if I'd had more time alone with her we could have worked things out. Jill looked like she was ready to spill her guts, to empty out everything she'd been holding onto, stuff I had no idea she'd been struggling with. I could see it now, though, clear as glass, and my heart went out to her even as I secretly wondered if Crew was right about the source of her sudden shift in attitude toward him.

Problem was, time was something I didn't have. As she opened her mouth to speak, hand rising to touch mine, a new voice interrupted and ruined everything.

"I hope you're not planning on letting a civilian make a mess of this crime scene." Robert strutted toward us in his puffy deputy's coat and bristling mustache, cowboy hat perched over his thinning hair, his jowls more pronounced than ever. He looked ten years older than me, these days, rather than the actual chronological six months between us, and I wasn't above smirking to myself love hadn't seemed to have treated him as well as it had me. Regardless, he seemed to think he had the upper hand, emerging from behind a curtain and I wondered how long he'd stood there, eavesdropping. Had he heard my nightmares admission? Who cared? Let him try to use anything I'd said against me, the snake. Still, his words and his appearance had the apparent desired effect on Jill because she instantly shifted from empathy to sullen frustration, snapping to attention and pointed at the big doors leading out into the main lobby.

"Time for you to go." She moved toward me, slow but actually threatening. I considered briefly testing her to see just how far she'd take things until I remembered her extremely physical proficiency from the self-defense class.

Instead, I chose cowardice and retreated, with a glare for Robert. He followed me, how delightful, leaving Jill behind in her solo guard of the ballroom turned fashion show catwalk, the smell of his revolting cologne making me gag.

"Just try and poke your nose in this time, Fanny." I spun toward him, ready to snap back, only to see that same darkness I'd witnessed in August, that flash of utter cruelty and desperate anger, rise in his gaze and thought better of it. He didn't seem to have the same reticence as he went on, leaning into me, the disgusting bristle of his heavy black mustache creeping me out. "You think you're having nightmares now? You don't know what a real nightmare is, missy. Trust me. You don't want to find out." He grinned, a tight and malicious expression, all yellowing teeth and chapped lips. "Push me, Fiona.

Do it. I promise, you'll regret it."

He did *not* just threaten me. I spluttered as he turned and reentered the ballroom, closing the door behind him, leaving me to fume ineffectually like a child chastised for misbehaving and left out in the cold.

We'd just see about that.

I should have gone home, gone back to Petunia's, gotten to work, excised my aggression in scrubbing toilets (about all Robert was worth to me at the moment). Instead, I found myself standing in Crew's office less than fifteen minutes later, the door only a second ago slammed behind me, my startled boyfriend leaping to his feet as I opened my mouth and began to rant.

I barely got two sentences out and I honestly don't recall what I said. I know Robert's name was in there, Jill's, and likely a threat back at that piece of trash who had an unfortunate bloodline tie to me I wished I could burn to the ground and never admit to again. Likely there was a death threat in it somewhere, too, though as red closed in around my vision and my blood boiled, my anger finally allowed out after a harried and breakneck drive down the mountain to be delivered to the man I loved, he broke his own rule to shut me down.

The moment his mouth met mine I melted, arms around his neck, though the raging fire of my anger didn't depart. If anything, it converted over from fury to passion and, as Crew stumbled backward in what was likely regret he'd locked lips with the she-devil he claimed to love in the first place, I pinned him against his desk and kissed him within an inch of his life.

I wasn't sure if he realized what he was getting himself into, breaking his no kissing at work rule like that, though I could understand on a rational level that he might have thought doing so would calm me down. Unfortunately, he miscalculated the scale of my utter frustration.

Thing was, instead of ending the kiss as I expected him to (and really, really hoped he wouldn't), he shocked me utterly by lifting me into his arms and carrying me to his chair. And though I was sure we'd be interrupted at any moment, we remained blissfully and passionately alone long enough for the kiss to run its course.

By the time I pulled away, heart pounding, sighing over his open mouth as that last breath of his filled my lungs, it was far too warm in the room. From the pink in his cheeks, he was thinking the same thing, pupils dilated so far there was barely any blue showing. I rested the tip of my nose against his, fingers wound through his hair, wishing we were at my place and only then feeling guilty we were in his office doing what I promised him we'd never do.

"No kissing at work," I whispered over his mouth.

"Exceptions at the sheriff's discretion," he growled back.

That made me laugh, and triggered one of his own, dispelling the last of my anger and setting my passion to simmer where it seemed to hover these days. I hated getting up but forced myself to do so, delighted his arms tightened around me a moment when I tried to rise the first time. But he sighed when I did and let me go, running his hands through his hair then over his face, the sound of skin rasping on stubble reminding me my mouth was still hot from his lips.

Fee. *Down* girl.

"I'm glad you're here." Crew winked slowly as I took a seat across from him, at a safer distance. He had to say it like that, right? Naughty thoughts had utterly replaced angry ones. Definitely an improvement but wasn't getting me any closer to doing what I'd promised Vivian I'd do. Something I was absolutely regretting as I let passion go and returned to the real world.

"What are we going to do about Jill?" Yes, we, damn it.

Crew leaned toward me and spoke, but he clearly ignored the question. "You were right to wonder about Libby Kim," he said. Not obvious about avoiding the elephant in the room or anything. I eye-rolled and let him. "She has no history as of eighteen months ago." He sat back again, frowning faintly at the file in front of him, a file he'd pushed toward me. I flipped it open and took a peek, but it only confirmed what he just said. "It's pretty clear she's not who she says she is."

"She might have had a grudge against Faith?" Possible, though why would she wait so long if she had murder in mind? "A hired killer?" Okay, that was a stretch. Still, she wasn't the bone-thin model type, looked pretty strong to me, in fact. She might have had the physical strength to hoist Faith's body via the ladder. But why make such a spectacle of the body? There had to be more to the story.

Crew didn't tell me I was nuts or give me any indication his agile mind hadn't gone down the same road. Instead, he stood, reaching for his jacket, blue eyes locked on me.

"I was just on my way to see the doc and find out what he knows," Crew said, gesturing at his door. "Feel like a trip to the morgue?"

I almost quipped I was more interested in a visit to his place but squashed that before it could emerge. There would be time to explore this rule-breaking version of the man I was in love with when murder wasn't hanging (literally) between us.

CHAPTER TWENTY-TWO

I stuck close to Crew despite the fact I'd been around enough dead bodies they really didn't bother me all that much anymore. At least, that was what I told myself as I shivered in the chill of the excessive air conditioning of the cheerily bright morgue where Dr. Aberstock grinned at us over the body of a dead guy I couldn't bring myself to identify by looking him in the face.

My mental chatter ran on and on as I tucked into my boyfriend's hip and did my best not to show the anxiety that grasped hold of me and shook me every so often. I wasn't expecting the place to be quite so white and chrome-filled, accustomed to the Hollywood look of such a space the reality of it seemed oddly worse. Surely it shouldn't have been this glaringly light, right? So scrubbed clean and shiny? A few shadows, a musty taint to the air, some kind of indication outside the repugnant tang of chemicals and cleaning agents that indicated dead people were in residence behind those shining silver drawer doors?

Mind you, I was actually more fascinated that grossed out, so you can make that mean what you want about me, because you can bet, I was judging, uh-huh.

"Definitely murder," Dr. Aberstock was saying while he hefted what looked like a liver onto a scale and checked the number on the digital display before calling out, "Three pounds, seven-point-eight ounces."

Barry logged the digits on a clipboard, the redundancy of the microphone recording everything despite his careful notes. He kept his head down, didn't comment on my presence, and I liked it that way.

"Kind of figured," Crew said, sounding so casual, so self-assured I relaxed somewhat and found myself staring into the wide-open cavity of the dead man's chest. Funny how seeing it on TV and in real life could be so incredibly different.

"Whoever strung that girl up used a stun gun on her first, to subdue her, I'm guessing." Dr. Aberstock winked at me over the rim of his reading glasses as he hefted the liver out of the tray and replaced it with what had to be the man's lungs. Yuck. "One pound, eight ounces."

Barry grunted something but didn't say it loud enough for me to make out ,so I chose to continue to pointedly ignore him.

"I can confirm TOD as 6:30PM," the doc went on, gloves caked in gore as he cheerily removed the lungs and finally set the gray brain on the scale. "Whoever killed her took a great risk, doing so in the early evening like that."

I'd been thinking the same thing, but Crew just grunted.

"Everyone was on dinner break," he said. "At least, according to Deputy Wagner. Including the crew. No one was supposed to be back on the stage until 8PM. It was just Alicia's bad luck she decided to do a check-in without Jill or Matt noticing." He talked about Jill in a calm, clear voice so maybe things weren't irreparable on his end. Still, he was professional enough not to show it to the doc, not to mention had to be wondering—like I was—how the victim and the murderer made it past the two security guards. Not to mention the murderer escaping followed by Alicia's entry.

Okay, phew, I was starting to wonder about Jill's skills myself. Except that there were two of them and four entrances to the ballroom. Way to defend my friend after the fact.

Dr. Aberstock shrugged at Crew's comment then peered at the scale. "Two pounds, seven ounces. Huh, nice sized noodle, there."

Someone loved his work just a bit too much.

Crew's phone rang and he turned away from me,

answering it, going to the far side of the room and leaning against a second exam table. He kept his voice down so I couldn't make out what he was saying and, uncomfortable with the silence, I chose to change the subject.

"Doc," I said, "what do you know about Vivian French's family?" The man had been my doctor when I was little, after all. He was a Reading resident through and through as far as I knew.

That's why I was a bit shocked when he responded, face turning down into a sorrowful frown while he paused, the brain heavy in one solid hand. "He was my first young loss after I moved here," he said, sounding like he'd taken the loss personally. "Poor boy, should never have happened." Dr. Aberstock tsked and set the brain aside, sighing while he peeled off his gloves. "Examination paused at 11:37AM." He turned off the microphone and leaned one substantial hip against the exam table, his Santa Claus face tilted to one side, rosy cheeks paling as he watched me. "Why do you want to know, Fee?"

"Just wondering," I said. "I thought I knew her, that's all." And him. I had no idea the doc wasn't a Reading native.

He nodded heavily, voice dropping to deep and kind as he spoke again, gesturing for Barry to join him at the body. The intern did, though he kept his head down and refused to look at me while the doc went on. "A tragedy, that family. What with Victor's loss at such a young age, then Ranier's in that terrible car accident. And with Martha suffering from dementia the way she does, Vivian has her hands full, that's for certain."

"How did Victor die?" I knew he'd drowned, something to do with a bee sting, at least according to the fake psychic, Sadie Hatch. But the circumstances evaded me. I was there, according to Mom. Why couldn't I remember?

Dr. Aberstock seemed to find that an odd question, reinforcing what Mom told me. "It was a tragic accident," he said, a strange tone to his voice. "He was stung by a bee, was highly allergic. Vivian said he slipped off the pier and couldn't swim. Fee, can't you remember?"

I shook my head, uncomfortable with the conversation, rubbing at the goosebumps on my arms as I backed away mentally, if not physically, though the temptation to do both was powerful. Instead, I hurried past that discomfort and into an epiphany that made me gasp. "Tell me about Siobhan Doyle."

Dr. Aberstock's bushy eyebrows shot up, blue eyes wide, pupils dilating a moment before he cleared his throat and exhaled like I'd shocked him with such a question. "You have a thing about ancient history today, my dear. That's a name I haven't heard in over thirty years." He recovered quickly, eyes narrowing. "You're full of hard questions, aren't you?"

I shrugged, feeling my hands tighten into fists in the front pockets of my jeans, the only shield I had against his prying tone. "There are too many secrets in this town, if you ask me."

I didn't mean to sound so whiny about it, but Dr. Aberstock laughed instead of chastising me, nodding, grinning.

"There are, dear Fiona, that much is true." He glanced sideways at Barry who seemed intent on sewing up the chest cavity of the dead man, the Y incision now folded back over the returned organs. "You know, I made your father a promise I'd never speak of Siobhan Doyle, not to you, not to anyone." He sounded sad all over again, eyes locked on the dead man. "Seemed so important to him back then, and I've kept that promise, but mostly because no one was looking for her anymore."

"Siobhan?" She'd gone missing?

When he met my eyes again, his were dark, shadowed with something he didn't want to say. "No. Her daughter. Fiona Doyle."

I couldn't breathe, couldn't draw an ounce of oxygen, hearing my name spoken so casually like that, knowing in my heart I was connected to this other Fiona in a way that would shake my whole world when I found out the truth. What Dad and Mom were hiding from me, what Malcolm and Siobhan wanted me to know.

Meanwhile, Dr. Aberstock went on as if he didn't notice my distress and I caught what he said through a haze of shock at hearing my own as he rambled on.

"As far as I'm concerned, what happened with Siobhan and her daughter had nothing to do with John." Oh my god, Dad. "It wasn't your father's fault, Fee, none of it." What? What wasn't? I wanted to lunge at the doc, grasp him by his shoulders, shake him. Instead, I was the one shaking, standing there, frozen, unable to move as he rubbed his round button nose and shrugged. "Your dad carries the guilt of it, Fee, but you have to know he did everything he could. And no matter what, Fiona's fate was on her." He tossed both hands, the pair of them landing on the metal table with a soft ringing sound as his wedding band impacted stainless steel. "John was a deputy himself, ten years into his career and he certainly didn't have any experience with that sort of thing. And he was too kind, you know? Too untried, while that waste of space sheriff, Harold Patterson, let the case go cold."

I fought to swallow, to ask the million or so questions I desperately wanted to ask. Instead, I gurgled loudly enough Dr. Aberstock broke out of his retrospective reverie and noted the state of me, I guess, because he instantly froze, then shook himself as if reminded of that promise he made to my dad so long ago.

"Let it rest," he said, circling the table to squeeze my hand. Something flashed in his eyes then, a fierceness I'd never seen before, as he leaned in and whispered, "Or, if you can't, for heaven's sake, find out what really happened to Fiona Doyle so your father can be free of his demons."

CHAPTER TWENTY-THREE

Crew's hand on my shoulder snapped me out of my deer in the headlights state. I immediately refocused on Dr. Aberstock, ready to demand more answers, only to find him retreating, waving at Barry who backed off the body while the doc examined his handiwork.

"Nicely stitched," he said with his jovial good humor returned like he hadn't just told me a fraction of what I needed to know and way more than anyone else in my life had about this particular mystery. I wanted to grill him, of course, I did, except as he looked up one last time and met my eyes I knew he was done, that I would get nothing else out of him, and that, yet again, I was on my own.

Except now I had a name, one eerily tied to mine,

to dive into.

Crew didn't seem to notice I was out of sorts, thanking the doc while my head spun. I barely heard him say goodbye, followed him on autopilot while I scoured my brain for the wherewithal to pull myself together long enough to stop shivering. It wasn't until we were in the cab of his truck Crew caught the hint and reached out to hug me. I clung to him, shaking for real now, while he chuckled in my ear.

"I never expected you of all people to be freaked out by the morgue." My boyfriend leaned away, grinning down at me. His expression shifted instantly as he realized there was more to it than the heebie-jeebies. Likely because I was crying and couldn't stop myself.

"I'm sorry," I hiccupped past the tears, wiping at the endless stream of them while Crew grabbed his tissue box, slightly crumpled from the passenger side floor, and handed it to me. I helped myself to multiples, fingers struggling to hold onto the soft sheets while I sobbed into them. "I'm so sorry, I don't know what's wrong with me." At least, that's what I tried to say. Still not sure if the meaning made it out or not past the choking tears.

Crew tucked me against him, cheek on my hair, rocking me softly and whispering things I'll never remember but that made me feel better, pulling me back from the brink of where Dr. Aberstock's lack of reveal took me. Fiona. That name, it had to have meaning, had to be connected to Dad, to me. Why else name me after a girl that vanished or died or who knew what else?

What happened to Fiona Doyle?

Crew's soothing did the trick and I righted myself a moment later, dabbing at the remaining tears, blowing my nose, apologizing while he watched me with those serious blue eyes, face still and empty of judgment.

"Did you want to talk about it?" He waited for me to answer, hand stroking my hair.

I shook my head after a moment of thought. I hadn't told him much—wait, if anything—about the mystery of Siobhan Doyle, partly I guess because of Malcolm Murray's involvement. And, because I had lived in fear for so long, since hearing about it, that Dad was responsible for something horrible, and I didn't want Crew to know. Yes, I was still protecting my father, but was it necessary? Not according to Dr. Aberstock. Still, until I knew more, I wasn't done being the good daughter, not after practically accusing my dad of cheating on my mom.

Did I say good daughter? Yeah, doing my best.

Crew looked like he was going to press, but instead sighed and looked out the window. "That was Liz," he said, "on the phone." I did my best not to react negatively to the fact his former partner, Special Agent Elizabeth Michaud, was still in the picture, though both of them had assured me there was never anything between them. Thing was, maybe not in Crew's case, but I had doubts Liz didn't have feelings for him at some point. Regardless, she still worked for the FBI, so that made her helpful, right? And I trusted Crew above anyone else until he proved otherwise.

Sheesh, Fee, way to tag on a caveat to the man who loved you unconditionally.

Crew filled me in as he started up the truck and pulled out of the parking lot, heading back toward Reading. The winding road leading from the new hospital toward downtown wasn't very well lit, a bone of contention during town meetings lately. I figured we were just lucky to have a hospital close at all and kept my mouth shut.

"Turns out Henry Ostler has been having some financial issues with a certain model." Crew turned on the heat, warmth helping me to stop shivering but doing nothing to erase the worry hovering in the back of my mind. I resolved to focus on what he was saying instead of what I was thinking as he went on. "Faith Leeman."

Interesting and enough to pull me the rest of the way back to the present and out of over thirty years in the past. Fiona and Siobhan had waited that long. They could wait a little longer. "What did he owe her for?"

"According to the court case she filed, he failed to pay her for a shoot she did," Crew said. "She used the proceedings to sever herself from his agency and go freelance. That was just before she joined Grace."

Sounded like possible motive to me. "Let's get his side of the story, then, shall we?"

Crew grinned, nodded, though there was a wickedness to it that made me pause. "Let's," he said.

Not like him to just invite me along like this, was it? I didn't argue, though, and it wasn't until we pulled into the parking lot at the lodge, I figured out what he was up to.

"You're using me against Jill." That almost made me angry, if she wasn't being a jerk about things and actually letting someone like Robert—and Rose through him—turn her against her friends.

Crew didn't respond, waiting for me outside the truck with his hands in his jacket pockets. I sighed over the duplicity of boyfriends who were also small-town sheriffs and joined him, hooking my arm through his as he headed for the front door.

"Go easy on her," I said at last, just as he pulled the big front entry open for me. "She's doing her best, Crew."

He didn't comment, though the normal warmth in his eyes was missing. So, they'd had the kind of words that weren't easily forgiven, had they? I wanted to shake him, too, wondering at my penchant for men and my need to rattle the living crap out of them. Dad was on that list, too, thanks, as I resigned myself to pissing Jill off further and joined Crew as he headed for the ballroom.

That meant he was looking for a confrontation. As we entered the crime scene, I held off judgment, though the sight of Jill talking with the very man I thought we'd come here to investigate made me wonder if Crew had set this up somehow. But nope, he looked disappointed enough I figured this was luck or the Universe or whatever doing its best to keep him from making a big mistake.

The expression on Jill's face told me she was in about the same mood as him when it came to Crew, though she snapped into professional when he did, nodding to both of us, face a tightly controlled mask as we came to a halt next to them. Henry seemed to notice the tension, though it was obvious he chalked it up to the case because when he spoke, he sounded livid.

"I understand the FBI has been investigating me." Whoops, though Crew didn't seem all that upset Henry knew that little detail.

"You've had some money problems with the victim, Mr. Ostler," the sheriff said, all casual, my favorite, that tone that told me Crew was in *underestimate me, I dare you* mode. There was something super sexy about him when he played quiet country cop that sent thrills through me.

Okay, fine, I admit it. Everything about Crew did that.

"You think that led to her murder, Sheriff Turner?" Henry's attempt at bluster came off fake and hollow. He had to have known we had the details of his court case with Faith.

"I understand you chose to contest Ms. Leeman's case against you." Crew almost came across as sympathetic, kind, even compassionate.

Henry hesitated, though it was obvious he wasn't a fool and saw right through the sheriff's attempt to put him at ease. But before he could answer, Jill spoke up, physically putting herself between Crew and the suspect.

I gaped as she shouldered herself into place and spoke in a low, angry voice.

"I've been instructed to tell the police that no one is to speak to you without a lawyer present." Um, hated to break it to her, but Jill was the police. What the hell?

Crew's face tightened, jaw jumping, that tic under his eye that used to be reserved for me making an appearance while the vein in his forehead pulsed. "This is the last time I'll warn you, Deputy Wagner." Whoa. I'd never heard that particular tone from him before. Not a threat, not anger, but the sort of utter conviction that made me choke up and want to turn and run away. "If you're going to continue to interfere with this investigation, to work contrary to the office you hold in your capacity as a security guard," everything he put into those two words made it absolutely crystal clear what he thought of her choice, "I would advise you to move on now, rather than waiting until one of those other jobs you've been applying for comes through. Because if I have to fire you, you will never get another position in law enforcement for the rest of your life, I promise you that."

I needed to do something, to stop this train wreck disaster barreling toward the inevitable. The pair of them glared at each other, Jill's anger more visibly volatile than Crew's, but no less frightening. Henry Ostler stared, glancing back and forth between them, even he seeming to realize he was in the middle of something he probably should back away from.

Jill finally backed down. I didn't see the moment of her choice. I was too busy looking at Crew. But when she did, it was with the level of resentment and guilt on her face that told me her days in Reading were numbered. Which hit me far harder than I was expecting.

I almost went after her as she turned and left the ballroom, almost. Would have, if Crew didn't immediately refocus his attention on Henry and start lobbing questions in a firm, low and intense voice that had the other man spluttering.

"I didn't pay her because I wasn't satisfied with her work." Henry finally got to the point, glancing nervously over one shoulder as if looking for backup and finding himself alone. I knew Crew would never actually hurt him, but even I felt intimidated by this frustrated and demanding man, a side of my love I'd never seen before, and I'd triggered a lot of sides in him over the years. "The photos taken that day were rejected by the client because Faith was combative and uncooperative. She disagreed, contested it, and we ended up in litigation. I should have won, except she pulled out the tears and batted those long lashes and the judge chose in her favor."

I was sure there had to be more to it than that, but Crew relented, nodded. Did he know something I didn't, something he hadn't told me?

"Any other money troubles?" Crew hadn't even bothered to take out his trusty notebook, hands on hips, blue eyes insistent.

"Nothing connected to Faith Leeman," Henry said, anger returning. "If you must know, that situation was all Grace's fault." Naturally, her ex would blame her, right? Men were pigs. All but the one standing next to me, that was. And my dad. Dr. Aberstock. Okay, enough blanket statements about men. Still. Oink.

"Henry," I said, "what was in the note Noel Lewder sent you?" I only had a scrap of the one Mila stole. Maybe he could shed light on the full contents.

He seemed surprised I knew but shrugged without any kind of sophistry visible. "She seems to think Faith set her up, drugged her the night she had her breakdown in New York." He sounded disdainful enough to be telling the truth.

"Do you think she had it in her to kill Faith?" It was a giant motive. Noel seemed devastated and I could only imagine what losing her livelihood and the job she loved meant to her. I know what it would have meant to me. Would I kill over it? No promises to the negative.

Henry seemed taken aback by that. "I'm not sure." He hesitated, then shrugged. "Possibly. Now that you mention it, she threatened both Grace and Faith in that note. The models can be so high strung." Wow, what a way to describe a murderer. Hey, I was high strung, right? "I can share it with you if you like." His eyebrows raised as he seemed to realize he was talking to me instead of Crew. "That is, with the sheriff."

Crew waved that off, bless him. "It would be helpful," he said. "Thank you for your cooperation."

But I wasn't done with Henry, not yet. In fact, my high-strung head was still thinking about what he'd said, heart speeding up a bit. "Could it be the wrong person was murdered that night?" Grace seemed to have a lot of enemies. "Or that someone is doing their best to ruin Grace?"

He froze, a flash of worry on his face, just enough I had an insight, a peek into the man's heart, and knew the truth that made me sad enough I relented on the pig analogy. "I wouldn't know," he said while my mind whispered he was still deeply in love with her. Did he know I knew? Regardless of his feelings, he pulled himself under control and shrugged.

"How about your private conversation with Libby Kim?" He flinched this time, visibly, while I watched him more carefully than before. "Grace won't be happy to hear her assistant has been spying on her."

Anger woke, softened instantly while Crew tensed beside me. Henry raised both hands, shook his head. "It's not like that." He swallowed hard before sagging just a little, shedding his arrogant powerhouse attitude a moment. "Libby is helping me… reach out to Grace."

"Why would you want to do that?" I already knew, didn't I? Crew's startled frown told me he didn't, though I guess heart matters were easy for guys to miss. Us girls? Yeah, all over that stuff like a bodice on a heaving bosom.

"It's personal." His voice sounded thick before he cleared his throat and spoke again, leaning in with his frown deepening. "If you'd like my guess as to who killed Faith…?" I nodded, Crew mirroring me, though Henry had locked eyes with me. "Of all the people who hated Faith Leeman," he said, "the most vocal was Mateo Marney."

"Why him?" I asked before Crew could, though my boyfriend didn't even flinch, still staring at Henry like he could wring truth from him just with his gaze alone.

"They'd talked about a partnership." Henry tossed his head like it was foolishness. "Faith thought of herself as an up-and-coming designer, but the poor child had no taste." Hmmmm. "From what I heard, Mateo invested a lot of money in developing a line with her, only to have Faith renege and try to claim the designs for her own."

CHAPTER TWENTY-FOUR

I stood outside Mateo's door, wanting to talk to Crew about his fight with Jill but not sure how to bring it up. He'd been stonily silent on the elevator ride, withdrawn and so far past stoic and into impenetrable fortress I hadn't known what to say or even if I should remind him I was there. Instead, I hugged myself and tried not to let the misery of watching my friend and my boyfriend lose their trust for each other over something I hadn't even been allowed to witness thanks to two people who really needed to take a flying leap off a cliff and splat to an unhappy end at the bottom.

Gruesome? You betcha. Well deserved, thank you very much. I was, after all, the queen of dead bodies, right?

Crew knocked firmly on Mateo's door. When I say firmly, I mean hard enough to make the lock rattle. Yup, he was definitely in a state, and I chose to err on the side of staying out of the way as the entry swung open and a partially undressed and rather mussed Mateo answered.

The designer looked flushed, rather sleepy, and I realized with a growing blush a redhead like me would never be able to hide in a million years he had good reason for his open shirt, his tousled hair, his half-lidded eyes. And his reason was slipping on her dress a bit too quickly for it to be a personal choice and not fed by guilt. The fact it was Kami Derham who'd been caught in this indelicate position did nothing to alter my opinion of her, though. Sure, she'd gossiped about him sleeping with Faith but apparently, she didn't have any qualms about chasing the dead woman's interests. He was handsome, and from the slow, sexy smile he fixed on me as he looked past Crew without a hint of self-consciousness, charming enough to get what he wanted from most women to boot.

Present happily girlfriended company excepted. Ahem.

"What can I do for you, Sheriff Turner?" Mateo's deep voice was a nice match for Crew's, though without the gravelly growl I was used to. His had more of a velvety softness to it, and the thread of a Spanish accent that made him sound all the more exotic.

"I need to speak with you about your business

dealings with Faith Leeman." Crew gestured toward the interior of the room, his own voice flat and unapologetic. "May I come in?"

"Please." Mateo stepped aside and I followed Crew, trying not to feel insulted he'd used the singular pronoun while reminding myself to be grateful he was letting me tag along in the first place. The handsome designer's dark eyes tracked me as I passed, and I felt myself blushing all over again.

"Matty," Kami said, adjusting her dress, beautiful face tightening into a rather unattractive scowl, "what is this about?" She showed zero indication she knew me, that she'd spent snack time in my kitchen or that she'd spilled seemingly spiteful information about the dead model and him, too.

He shrugged, joining us, reaching out to run his fingertips down her cheek to the point of her chin. "Faith and I were working things out," he said, like it was no big deal.

It obviously was to Kami whose eyes flared wide, her mouth dropping open. Wait, hadn't she said he and Faith were an item? Clearly, she'd been trying to deflect, then. Did that put her higher on the suspect list? I didn't get to question her about it. She called him a rather unflattering name I wouldn't repeat in polite company before slamming out of the room but giving me the impetus to elevate her on my own list of sorts. If she had a love triangle issue with Mateo and Faith, that could have been motive after all. Love made people do weird things. I should know.

"You and Ms. Leeman had a relationship?" Crew

seemed to be relaxing again somewhat. At least, I took it that way when he pulled out his notebook and started writing, pausing as he waited for Mateo to answer.

The designer shrugged again, sinking to the bed and leaning back on both hands, bare chest nicely muscular, fully exposed as he winked at me from that suggestive pose. "If you can call it that," he said, far more casually than he should have. "I've slept with most of the girls, to be honest. Can you call that a relationship?"

Crew's whole body tensed. "A business relationship," he said, flat and harsh.

Mateo laughed. "Ah, that," he said. "Again, we were working things out."

I somehow doubted this casually sexual man could muster the kind of anger needed to hang someone, but then again, who knew what hid behind those dark eyes, that languid smile? And he was clearly in great shape, muscular chest flexing. "What did she have on you, Mateo?"

He flinched ever so slightly before laughing again, only this time his eyes weren't so soft. "Oh, her list, you mean?"

List? "You know what I mean." At least one of us did, and I was only now kicking myself it was important, and I'd dropped the ball entirely. Kami mentioned a list, right? That Faith used it as leverage against others. Had I forgotten to tell Crew? Apparently. He glanced at me with a tight jaw and a question in his eyes that told me I'd failed to mention information I had he didn't. And, crap.

Mateo stood, buttoning his shirt, suddenly all business. "It's true, she kept a list of secrets she used as leverage against those she wanted things from. But she had little against me, mostly trysts I'd had with married women." He actually yawned. "Boring, and ineffective."

"Where is it now?" Again I thought a list like that would be excellent motive for murder, depending what was on it and who considered their secrets worth killing for.

He tucked in his shirt like we didn't even exist, reaching for a dress jacket he slipped on, checking his reflection in the mirror. "I have no idea. But, if you find it, let me know?" He laughed one more time before focusing on Crew. "I'd love a peek for my own purposes." That wink, seriously.

"Where were you at 6:30PM yesterday?" Crew sounded like he could care less. Had he written off Mateo as a suspect? Not like him. Then again, maybe his attitude was an attempt to get under the man's skin. And when the designer reacted with a frown of his own, I understood my boyfriend's brilliance and felt a surge of pride at his cleverness.

Ego tweaked by someone treating him as if he didn't matter, Mateo bristled. "I was with one of the help, a maid, I think. And no, I don't know her name. But she should be on video with me near the kitchen." He grinned, leered, really, and I found myself asking when and why I'd even remotely considered him attractive. Just *ew*. "We had some fun in the storage closet."

Creep.

We left the lodge, heading for downtown, me fuming over the vile nature of men and Crew silent as he fought his own inner struggle. When we passed the town sign, I sighed and realized it wasn't Mateo who'd made me irritable. I owned up to the underlying worry that plagued me and, in a moment of inspired action, blurted everything I knew about Siobhan Doyle into the silent cab of my boyfriend's truck.

He didn't speak, didn't react much, either, to his credit. Just listened as I unloaded and cried a little and told him what I knew. Not much, though my worries about Dad were paramount and pretty clear as Crew pulled up in front of Petunia's and parked, engine still running, while I told him what Dr. Aberstock said to me only a little while ago, filling in the rest of what I'd discovered in this achingly unusual mystery.

Crew turned to me, face still and expressionless and I instantly feared he was furious with me. I'd kept this from him when I should have told him everything. But, instead of being angry, he reached out and pulled me against him until I was tucked into his arms, my favorite place to be these days, the warm air from the truck's heater on both of us, my heart beating in time with the man I loved so very much.

"Do you want me to look into it for you?" He was asking. Wow. Since when did he ask?

"No, please." I snuffled and wiped at my nose with the back of my hand, accepting yet another tissue from him. Sheesh, I had to stop the waterworks, or he'd need a new box before too long. I picked at the corner of the sheet as I exhaled the worry I'd been harboring into the quiet air of the cab, feeling better already just for having shared. I blinked and smiled up at him, the tears in my lashes making him waver in front of me, though it was impossible to miss the love in those blue eyes. "I've come this far. And now I have somewhere new to look. It's an old mystery, Crew. I promise, when I find out more, I'll tell you."

He nodded, kissed me. "Thanks for telling me," he said. "It means a lot to me, that you trust me enough." Crew looked away, cleared his throat, swallowed a couple of times. Wow, was he getting choked up? I hugged him hard and felt his arms tighten in response. "Do you think your dad did something illegal?"

"Not according to the doc," I said, clinging to that fact. I trusted Dr. Aberstock. If he said Dad wasn't at fault, whatever happened, he wasn't. But since Dad blamed himself, he was clearly involved in what did go down.

"That's enough for me." Crew let me go, sighed, kissed me again. "You need anything, let me know?" Was that a request? Sounded like one. "Thanks for coming with me. I needed you there today." He paused. "Jill." Like her name was explanation enough.

It kind of was. "Did you want to talk about what happened?"

His turn to shake his head, though he smiled faintly instead of crying like I did. "We both said things we didn't mean and now it's too late to take them back. The details of them don't matter, Fee. It was the intent behind them that cause the hurt." Crew stretched a bit, both big hands settling on the steering wheel as he let me go. "I'll deal with it. I just hate to see Jill go like this, when it's not about her, really."

No, it was about Robert and Rose, right? I grit my teeth and scowled through the windshield, wishing Rosebert were out there right now, standing in front of the bumper of Crew's truck. Honestly, I would have hit the gas and not felt a second of regret.

Okay, maybe a second. Bodywork was expensive, yo. Snort.

I leaned in and took my own turn kissing him, which evolved into a bit more intensity than I had planned, until I was breathless and feeling much, much better about the whole day. From the sparkle in Crew's eyes, I'd been as helpful to him as he was to me.

I waved as he drove off, dumping my coat at the sidebar as I checked the guest listings and found everything in order. It was long enough after lunch things should have been quiet for the remainder of the afternoon, and I had some research to do. So, with my heart again in my throat and growing tension keeping my attention, I slipped down to my apartment to fetch my laptop, stumbling at the bottom of the stairs in the dim quiet, pausing to flick on the light.

And letting out a screech of terror at the sight of Mila sitting on my couch, patting my pug, smiling at me.

CHAPTER TWENTY-FIVE

My first impulse was to call Crew. Why the hell hadn't I asked him to arrest her in the first place? I'd taken a soft stance on the crazy woman who lurked in the silence in my private space like a spider waiting to pounce, hugging my pug who seemed at ease and happy despite the fear racing through my veins.

I think Mila must have realized she'd made a huge misstep, likely the first time in her life she actually figured out she was missing the regular social graces that kept most folks from breaking into other people's houses with the intent of scaring the living crapola out of them. She surged to her feet, both hands outstretched, a tight and worried smile on her face while I clasped at my throat with one hand, the other hunting in my pocket for my phone.

"Fee, it's okay, please, you don't have to worry." She sounded so soothing, like I was a stray dog she needed to calm before she could throw a rope around my neck and drag me off to who knew where to do who knew what to me. "It's fine, I'm sorry, I didn't mean to scare you."

Her tone was working, my pounding heart slowing down, and I chalked my reaction up to the day I'd had, thanks, finally letting go of the paralyzing fright that gripped me in favor of a surge of anger.

"You shouldn't be down here." I turned and jabbed a finger at the stairs, shaking all over again and tired of it. "I'm going to have to ask you to leave, Mila, and I don't just mean my apartment. You have to go, now. Or I'm calling the sheriff and having you removed."

As her big eyes flooded with tears, her sunken cheeks hollowing as her mouth opened and she released a wail of despair, I finally admitted to myself what I'd suspected all along, what I didn't want to believe. That Mila had transferred her dedicated obsession for Willow Pink not to Grace, but to me.

Oh, crap.

"I love you," she whispered, sobbed, falling to her knees at my feet, grasping my free hand and pressing it to her cheek. "Please, Fee, I just want to help. I'll do anything for you." She met my eyes again, her tears gone, feverish expression almost worse than finding her down here, waiting and smiling and petting Petunia in the silence. "*Anything.*"

So, any sane person would have immediately

called for said sheriff boyfriend, right? And had the crazy girl evicted from the premises, likely in handcuffs and with a one-way ticket booked back to the mental hospital where she'd spent her previous many months. Yup, any sane person.

Me? Was it wrong when Mila's mouth opened and she said the word *anything* my mind stuttered and for an instant—okay, for longer than an instant, I fess up—I wondered if I could use her obsession to my advantage.

Oh, Fee. Fee, Fee, Fee.

"Mila." I helped her to her feet, squeezing her hands, doing my best to hide the fact she was seriously freaking me out while hating myself for even considering mentioning to her what I was about to mention to her because I was a horrible, horrible person.

"Yes, Fiona?" She blinked at me, wavered in front of me, clinging to me, to my every word.

"There is something you can do for me." I was going to hell. H-E-double hockey sticks. And no one was going to be able to save me.

Mila shivered and beamed like a beaten puppy finally receiving the praise she so desperately longed for. "*Anything.*" She stressed that again, madness behind her eyes and I swallowed before signing my one-way trip to the eternal fires.

"There's this list…" And, with remorse but the determination of the condemned, I told her about Faith's blackmail details.

Mila nodded immediately, squeezing my fingers

so tightly I knew they'd tingle from the return of circulation. "Smart," she said, voice oddly lucid and utterly sane though her face held nothing of the sort. "I'd do the same, in her position. I'll find it for you, Fee. If it's the last thing I do."

She didn't wait for me to try to stop her—yes, I knew I should try to stop her—but bounded up the steps and through my door. Her footsteps crossed the foyer, the front doorbell ringing as she left, and I exhaled shakily while my pug sat on my foot and yawned with a meowing sound that made me wince.

"She won't find it," I said, while Petunia watched me with those big, empty brown eyes devoid of anything judging or unhappy. "I just gave her something to do until this is over and Crew can arrest her." Yeah, nice try, Fee. Thing was, that list was likely the best evidence we had to catch Faith's murderer. And if the murderer had it in their possession, the likelihood we'd find it was pretty slim.

But someone like Mila? Yup, going to hell. Sigh.

I returned upstairs, wanting the company of someone, anyone, after the encounter with the crazy lady and hoping to track down Mom or Daisy and cling to them for a minute. Noise in the kitchen drew me inside, and, expecting to pour my worries out on my mother, I slumped unhappily through, struggling with the demon of setting Mila Martin loose with a job to do and no real parameters to keep her in check.

I was startled to find, not my mother after all, but

Noel Lewder hovering in the kitchen. She stood in front of the open fridge door, staring into it, the light making her gaunt face appear goblinesque. After a second of surprise, I joined her, embracing this chance to talk, to do some snooping, hoping it would ease the guilt I struggled with over sending a clearly troubled woman out to do something likely illegal.

Noel noticed me almost immediately, shutting the door with a thud, guilt written on her own face as if looking for food was the ultimate in shame. "Sorry," she said, rubbing both upper arms with her hands, clearly unhappy. "I missed lunch."

She looked like she skipped enough meals. Compassion won, like it usually did, and a moment later I was fishing leftovers out of the fridge, offering her options. She settled on the remains of a salad, clearly a vegetarian as she flinched away from every offering of meat I shared, though she devoured a small ball of goat cheese in two bites.

"I didn't mean to be rude earlier." Noel swallowed around her chewing, eyes down. "I'm just frustrated. My career was ruined, and no one seems to care." She blinked, big eyes full of tears. That was the second huge gaze aimed at me in the last little bit, not to mention my own crying feeding my empathy. I nodded and nibbled a cookie I'd liberated from the tin on the top shelf, loving the cold of the chocolate chips, reminding me of sneaking treats from Mom's carefully preserved caches when I was a little girl.

"I get it, Noel," I said. "I really do. You chose a tough career. I don't envy you at all, being in the limelight like that. It has to take its toll."

She shrugged those narrow shoulders, her collarbone standing out in sharp detail under her skin, so thin the bony ridges of her breastbone caught shadows. I wanted to feed her something more substantial than salad and a bit of cheese, but she seemed content with the offering, turning down a cookie when I held out the still-open tin. Might have helped myself to a couple more just in reaction to her emaciation. Might have.

"I love modeling," she whispered, voice cracking. "I love everything about it. It's not fair I've had to give up my life because of someone else's decisions."

"Did you know about Faith's list?" I didn't mean to just jump in like that, but it was on my mind for obvious reasons while I pondered in vague panicked horror what I'd done, sending Mila out there looking for it like I had. What was wrong with me? I had to tell Crew what I'd done.

Noel, meanwhile, was nodding. "We all did." She sounded bitter enough about that to catch my attention and distract me from my need to call my boyfriend and confess I'd set loose a wild woman on our shared case. Eep.

"Do you have one of your own?" Would make sense, right?

But Noel shook her head, sighed over her salad she now just picked at with her fork before setting that aside and rubbing her hands over the thighs of her jeans. "I never played that game," she said, sounding like she regretted it now. "I thought about it. Most of the girls keep their own lists, you know. For protection, mostly small stuff. But I just couldn't bring myself to be that person." Did she think that led her here, to this fate? From her angrily twisted lips, yes.

"Do you know what was on Faith's list?" Noel might be able to give me what I needed without Mila. That would be a big relief and would mean I could have Crew arrest her before anything bad happened. Because something bad was going to happen, I just knew it.

But Noel shook her head, though she didn't mention Faith's list when she spoke next. "I had one piece of information, and one only," she said, eyes intense, hands shaking, lower lip trembling. "And it got me here."

"What did you find out?" I wanted to pat her hand, to tell her it was going to be okay. She seemed so frail, so vulnerable and I just couldn't bring myself to judge her. She'd made her choices, no matter where they'd led her, against Grace or not. There was just too much hurt in her for me to find her anything but sad.

"You'll think I'm a suspect in her murder." Noel started to cry, hands over her eyes. "But I swear I didn't kill her." She dropped her fingers, tears leaking down her thin face, so open and utterly exposed I believed every word she said. "Faith was selling drugs to the other girls. And when she found out I knew, she ruined me."

CHAPTER TWENTY-SIX

It took me a moment to process, but when I finally did I gasped. "She was a drug dealer?"

Noel nodded, misery on her face, slumping over the remains of her salad. "I don't do drugs, I swear it. I abhor them. My sister died of an overdose when she was fifteen." There was the hurt again, rancor. "We were models together, the two of us. But she got into drugs to stay thin, and I couldn't stop her." Noel was crying all over again, though clearly audible and understandable, unlike me when I wept. "I would never take anything, ever. Not after what Chrissy went through." I nodded to encourage her to go on and she did, sniffling, wiping her tears on her hands then on her jeans. "I'm positive it was Faith who set me up and got me arrested." She shrugged, looked away. "She made it look like I was the dealer, slipped me drugs so I had that meltdown on the runway. I barely remember it." She shuddered. "All I do remember is feeling like my skin was crawling off and I had to fix it. I've never been so terrified in my life. Like everyone in the crowd was laughing at me, waiting for that dress to devour me." Holy, that sounded utterly nightmarish. No wonder she freaked out. "The police let me go because they didn't have any proof aside from the drugs in my system. But Henry dropped me, no one else would touch me. All because I found out Faith was selling."

"That sounds like an excellent murder motive, Noel." It was only fair to play straight with her. And it worked. She shrugged one more time, her hair escaping the ponytail keeping it back from her face, long strands falling forward that she pushed away with impatient hands.

"I know," she said, suddenly desperate, with an ache in her voice that made my chest hurt. "I get that, I told you. But I didn't do it. Besides," she tossed her head, face set into a flare of rage, "if I was going to kill Faith, I'd do something more direct. Like stuffing her own drugs down her throat. Not hanging her with that dumb dress."

More direct, huh? "How about using a stun gun?"

Noel didn't seem to notice I'd dropped a hint and I covered my wince with a bite of cookie. "Kami has one of those," she said, casual, distracted as she stared into the remains of sad salad on her plate. "So does Libby."

Libby again. "What do you know about her, her past?" Noel was being forthcoming, so I might as well take full advantage. Because hell and all, I was going, right? Might as well just rifle around for gossip when this poor girl was at her most vulnerable.

Sorry. Not sorry.

"I don't," Noel said. "No one does, as far as I can tell. She's always been pretty secretive about where she came from and all. She works for Grace, so maybe she knows?"

"Did Faith ever act like she had anything on Libby?" I didn't trust the assistant, her missing background making her my prime suspect.

Noel perked at that, nodding without her broken hurt so visible this time, like helping was giving her what she needed. The parallel to Mila wasn't lost on me but I just sighed and listened to her response.

"I don't know what," she said, "but Faith claimed to have dirt on Libby, now that you mention it. And whatever Libby's hiding?" She shivered, rubbing her thin arms brusquely. "No one crosses her. No one. She's scary."

Not hard evidence, per se, but following the line of my own suspicions sufficiently it was good enough for me.

Mom's bustling arrival interrupted us, her harried expression smoothing out at the sight of Noel. Weird, Mom was never late, dinner's pre-prep not even started. Come to think of it, she was usually here all day. Where had she been? The worried look on her face made me pause on my way to seek out

Libby.

"Anything I can help with?" Mom rarely showed it when she was concerned.

She just patted my hand and put on her apron, Petunia eagerly hanging out at her feet in turn, abandoning Noel whose tiny bites garnered little in the way of falling crumbs.

"It's fine," she said. "Your father's just away on a case and I worry."

Huh. He was supposed to be running security here for me. Nice of him to tell me he was leaving town. "Is he okay?" Maybe I should have been more worried about him than less, but Dad could take care of himself.

"Absolutely." Okay, that amount of faked assurance made me nervous. But Mom wasn't talking any further, smiling at Noel and actually putting her to work. I left the kitchen and headed back to the lodge, my in-transit call to my father ending at his gruff voice telling me to leave him a message.

Grunt. Fine. I'd call back later. Right now, I had a suspect to question.

Libby was easier to find than I expected, hanging out in the coffee shop near the ski lift, another new addition of Alicia's to the White Valley Lodge. I slipped into the seat next to the scowling young woman, pinning her against the window as I tucked into the bench and offered a bigger than necessary smile.

I wasn't exactly trying to comfort her. Nope, it was my intention instead to rattle her if possible.

Because at this point, I was rather over the whole business and really wanted to get back to my life, thanks. There was just too much going on around me for the full enjoyment of murder mystery solving to take hold.

Did I just call murder enjoyable? Oh, Fee.

"Tell me what Faith had on you," I said without preamble, still smiling.

Libby's dark brows pulled together, and she looked away after her initial startled response to my sudden appearance. "I don't have to tell you anything."

Sullen, huh? I could do sullen. I poked her with one finger, doing my best not to shake her, actually, and proud of myself for holding it together. Because grinning maniacally at a murder suspect while pinning her down and prodding her for a confession was holding myself together. You betcha.

"I know about Faith's list." Libby didn't even flinch, so she must have gotten that from my initial question. "And I know she had enough on you to make you nervous. That's motive for murder." Okay, a stretch, fine. But the young woman's twitch of guilt wasn't lost on me. "Were you supplying her with drugs?"

"Whatever," she said, looking away again, staring into her coffee cup. "Think what you want. But I had nothing to do with any of it. I work for Grace. That's it."

Argh. Totally the wrong attitude to take with me at the moment. But before I could go all Mom on her and dissect her with my weighty older woman vibes, someone else did it for me.

Grace appeared, slipping into the bench seat across from us, not looking at me. Instead, she fixed her eyes on Libby with her own face creased in worry.

"Lib." The young woman flinched this time, hardcore, refusing to look at her boss, shivering a little. "Please. I know you didn't kill Faith. But you have to tell me what you're hiding. I can't protect you if you won't talk to me."

This sounded like an old conversation I'd dropped myself in the middle of and from the strained look between the pair I was right about my guess. I might as well not have been there at all as Libby finally met her boss's eyes and exhaled, leaning in to grasp Grace's hand with one of her own, so tightly the skin whitened at the knuckles.

"I never meant to involve you, Grace, I swear." Libby sounded close to tears while the older woman cupped her hand with her free one and showed no sign if the desperate grasp hurt or not. "I just needed a job, a place to hide out for a while. I didn't want anyone else to suffer for my past."

"You can tell me anything," Grace said in that level, warm tone that was both maternal and friendly and so far from what I'd mastered I let her have the moment. "Anything. I won't judge. You know me better than that by now."

Libby nodded, misery clear on her face and for the first time I watched her lower her guard and let

Grace in. And, in doing so, let me in, too.

"Despite what you might think, (was that aimed at me or Grace? Didn't matter) this has nothing to do with Faith. She thought she knew what I was hiding, but she had no real idea. None." Libby was shaking for real by now, her lower lip trembling, tears welling and falling down her cheeks to splash on the tabletop. Grace reached out and liberated a few napkins, handing them over, while the young woman sniffled and pulled herself into order enough to go on. "I'm not a murderer, but I'm related to some."

Wow, what?

Grace glanced at me and, in that brief instant of eye contact, told me I was to remain utterly silent and under no circumstances was I to interfere. Amazing how much information could be transferred from one person to another in the flash of a glance. I held perfectly still and waited Libby out while her boss simply sat there and held her hand.

Libby choked on her next words before shaking her head and sagging forward, sobbing softly into the handful of napkins. "My family," she finally managed, voice thick, rough. "I'm hiding from my family. If they find me, they'll kill me."

My heart palpitated while I fought empathy at her admission. Understanding rode a wild horse through my mind while Grace's dismay turned to compassion.

"Tell me," she said, firm, warm but demanding.

Libby didn't protest at all, simply lowering the napkins so she could speak, tears an endless trickle to join the puddle on the table. "My real name is Eve

O'Shea," she whispered, "only daughter of Patrick O'Shea, youngest son of the Chicago O'Sheas. The crime family."

Yikes. The names didn't mean anything to me but being on the wrong side of organized crime wasn't anything to sniff at.

"Libby," Grace said, paused. "Eve." She squeezed and the young woman squeezed back. "Why did you run away?"

"My father was trying to force me to marry the son of one of his competitors to join the families together." Libby/Eve sniffled, wiped at her nose, her tears finally slowing as indignant anger took over. "When I ran, I betrayed him, betrayed everyone. But I couldn't live like that, not anymore. I escaped and went to New York and reinvented myself. Found you." She blinked at Grace. "At first, I just needed you as a cover, to create a new life. I didn't mean to put you in danger, I swear. I was only going to stay a few months, to give myself some backstory. Then I was going to move on." She exhaled softly, shook her head. "But you're awesome, Grace, and every time I planned to tell you I was leaving it seemed like terrible timing. You needed me." She sobbed one more time, silent and heartbreaking. "I should have left before it was too late. But now it is and you're in danger because I didn't go when I should have."

What did that mean? I had an uncomfortable flash of insight that made me want to throw up suddenly, but instead of prodding that particular line of thought, I blurted something much more immediate.

"Where were you when Faith was killed, Libby?" I winced and almost called her Eve, but the young woman was already speaking, to Grace, not to me, but at least she was still talking.

"I don't have an alibi." Her thin shoulders rose and fell in defeat. "I was hiding in my room."

"Why?" I already knew the answer, wanted to deny it, but couldn't. I had enough intimate connection to the reason for her need to escape to let myself be surprised when she answered.

"One of my father's men is here," she said, empty and hopeless. "When he showed up at the lodge, I knew I had stayed too long with you."

I swallowed while Grace's fingers lifted, stroked the last of the tears from the girl's cheek. "We'll deal with this together. I'll do everything I can to keep you safe, I swear it." She met my eyes, hers full of anxious worry. "Can we have the sheriff put her in protective custody?"

I nodded, not sure if he could or would, but prepared to go to bat for exactly that if necessary. "Libby," I said, knowing my own voice sounded hollow and devoid of emotion, "the man you saw, the one you're afraid of. What's his name?"

The young woman met my eyes at last, and, tone dull with fear, said, "Malcolm Murray."

CHAPTER TWENTY-SEVEN

I reached out to Libby before thinking, covering Grace's hand with mine in a pyramid of female support while wondering how I could have ever thought the clearly terrified young woman could have been a murder suspect. How had I missed the obvious signs of buried horror, the reflexive retreat like a build-in flinch from life? Because I'd been set on blaming someone for the death of Faith so I could move on already.

Huh. Not like me to treat murder so lightly. I really either had to choose to back away from the death game or commit totally. Wait, was that Dad's problem with me? Why he didn't share? Because I wouldn't commit to his business? I felt my insides shrivel slightly while I spoke up in an attempt to reassure the scared and ready to rabbit Libby/Eve.

"Malcolm is my problem," I said, knowing now why he'd been here. Not for me, but that business he mentioned. Libby. Eve. Damn it, not in my town. "Let me deal with him."

She stared at me, wide-eyed. "You know him?"

"Let's just say I have something I can leverage against him." Just let him try to hurt this young woman on my watch. If he wanted answers like he claimed he did, answers for Siobhan I now believed were tied to her daughter, Fiona, he'd be backing the hell off, orders from his bosses or not.

She swallowed, looked away, clearly disbelieving. "Check the video footage," she whispered, returning to stare into her coffee cup. "I should be on it going to my room. I didn't come out again until Grace called me."

I'd take that as an alibi. "Thank you for trusting me," I said.

She shook her head then, looking up at Grace who smiled faintly, kindly. "Not you," she said.

Point taken.

I paused, knowing I'd built a bit of cred and not wanting to eliminate it entirely, but needing confirmation despite what Henry told me. "Libby, why were you talking with Henry Ostler on Sunday morning?"

Grace froze, stared at her assistant, then me, with enough hurt in her eyes I wished I'd kept my mouth shut.

Libby sagged, squeezing her boss's hands. "We

need to talk," she said. "I know you're hurting but I believe him, Grace." Compassion? Now? Wow, she was a better person than I'd given her credit for. "Henry still loves you."

Whoops. I hadn't meant to get in the middle of this and when tears welled in Grace's eyes, I knew it was time for me to go. Nothing to do with murder here, and affairs of the heart weren't my job at the moment. At least not Grace's.

I left the pair talking quietly and hurried back to town, to the sheriff's office, rushing into Crew's presence with growing unease in my heart. I spilled what Libby had told me, taking in his surprise then grim nodding as he retreated to his desk to take notes. But when I wrapped up with her possible innocence being recorded for posterity, he made a face that told me it wasn't so neat and tidy just yet.

"Turns out there's no actual footage." Crew's grimace reached the corners of his blue eyes as he rocked back in his chair, the wood creaking faintly under his weight.

Just what we needed. "The killer found a way to sabotage the cameras?"

His lips twisted, a wry grin. "Nothing so nefarious," he said. "Mundane, unfortunately. Turns out something went wrong with the whole system. Alicia contacted the company and found out they were tracking a glitch in their programming. So, just a tech issue, but still problematic."

I groaned and sank back myself, staring at the small stain on the hardwood floor under the corner of the desk near my foot, scowling at it like the blot under the old varnish was an intentional mark against us. "Great, so no proof either way, for any of our suspects."

Crew shrugged, sitting forward with his muscular forearms, bared to the elbows where he'd rolled his sleeves back, resting on the cluttered surface of his desk. His long, strong fingers toyed with a pen as he spoke. "It certainly doesn't help us narrow things down."

"Well, I'm counting Libby out, if that's worth anything." I scowled at my bobbing foot, crossed over one knee, knowing the motion was pure agitation and forcing it to stop out of stubbornness only to have it start up all over again the moment I switched focus. Sigh. "She's scared, Crew, but not of being caught as a murderer. And she was certain the footage would exonerate her, with no way of knowing it wouldn't be available."

He didn't change expressions, though when he spoke it was clear he was trying not to ruffle feathers. "I'm sure you're right," he said, "but we can't discount anything just yet, Fee. You know that."

In other words, I'd been wrong in the past enough times he couldn't trust my gut, though I always seemed to end up on the right (or was that wrong?) end of the real murderer. Lucky me.

"You're also forgetting to mention she had excellent reason to kill Faith if she was terrified for her life." He pointedly locked gazes with me, though again not confrontational, steady and ready for my reaction. "If she thought Faith was going to turn her in to her family, protecting her own life by taking the model's makes perfect sense, sweetheart."

I hesitated, blushed, grinned. "You just called me sweetheart."

Crew's lips parted, teeth flashing as he smiled back, eyes sparkling. "I guess I did."

Insert warm, fuzzy, happy moment here.

It passed faster than I would have liked, but I did my best to cling to it as my boyfriend exhaled and dropped the pen he'd been assembling and disassembling in a steady twist of the barrel. "Turns out Mateo Marney's alibi is good," he said, sounding like he wished it was different. The designer's blasé attitude about his sexual conquests really seemed to stir up something unhappy in Crew. "Jill found the maid he'd been with, and she admitted she'd been indiscreet." He sighed again. "Alicia said she has to fire her now. Sucks all the way around, poor kid."

I was with him in judging the handsome Mateo for taking advantage of the girl, though in all honesty, I'd known enough young ladies in my day who were more than happy to dally with exotic strangers I couldn't be entirely sure the designer was totally at fault.

Wow, when had I turned into a prudish old lady? Oh yeah, when I'd moved into my grandmother's bed and breakfast, adopted her fat, farting pug and chose to make Reading home.

"What about Kami Derham?" I chewed my bottom lip, replacing foot bobbing with that new abuse. "She was pretty quick to blabbermouth about everyone else and had zero qualms about gossiping. Maybe in an effort to shift blame from her to others? After all, Noel said she owned a stun gun."

Crew mused over that a moment. "Worth chatting with her again," he said, standing and grabbing his coat. "You heading home?"

I should have. I'd just been at the lodge, after all, and I really needed to go back to Petunia's and get some work done. That's why, logically, I found myself in the cab of Crew's truck, driving back up the mountain with his big hand in mine. Because I wanted to be with him, though, right? Sure, that was the reason. Maybe my distracted mind had led me a bit astray earlier, but here I was, right back in the thick of the investigation, nose quivering with curiosity.

The only trouble, of course, was we weren't the first ones to reach Kami with the information I thought only we'd uncovered.

That's why it was so shocking to find Robert interrogating her, the model seated, shivering and wide-eyed, in a chair while my asshat cousin loomed over her, a bully through and through. Not that the bullying was shocking. Just the fact he'd managed to put two and two together and not get five.

"You're just in time to watch me solve this case." He jabbed his thumb in Kami's direction, smirking at his boss, ignoring me completely. "I'm sure the council will love to hear of your continuing incompetence."

I almost sighed and eye-rolled. Took a massive effort on my part not to. Crew, on the other hand, merely looked down at Kami with kindness on his face and in his voice.

"I have a few questions for you, Ms. Derham," he said.

Robert's snarl was audible as he spun on her as if to get the jump on Crew. "Where is it?" He snapped the question like she should know exactly what he was talking about. "Where is your stun gun?"

She gaped up at him, tears in her huge eyes, lips opening and closing but only squeaks emerging.

Crew turned to his deputy, face level and still, but that set to his shoulders that told me he wasn't happy Robert had this information. Was he withholding from his staff now? How much pressure was my boyfriend under he couldn't trust either of his deputies? But instead of saying anything against Robert as I expected him to, Crew instead addressed Kami while staring right at my cousin. "Please answer the question, Ms. Derham."

She blubbered a moment, shaking her head, her long hair hanging out of the tidy ponytail at the nape of her neck, pieces escaping as if she'd been disheveled in some way. If Robert was roughing her up Crew would have his ass on a plate.

"I don't know," she finally forced out, barely audible. "It's missing."

Robert didn't wait for Crew to act, whipping out his phone instead and pushing it in her face. I caught the image of something on the screen but wasn't close enough to make out what it was. All good, he was about to tell me.

"I found a picture of you with it on your social media." He sounded pretty damned proud of himself while he forced her to stare at the image he showed her. "And I matched the model to the one that stunned Faith before she was killed. What do you have to say about that, Ms. Derham?"

Kami's eyes met mine, hers overflowing with fear. "I didn't do anything!" And then she buried her face in her hands and started to sob while Robert reached for his handcuffs.

"That's all the proof I need." He was closing in on her when Crew stepped between them. The sheriff didn't say anything, just moved enough to block Robert from cuffing the model. For a long moment the two faced off, Crew silent, watchful, Robert blustering and huffing until he spoke again, resentment so obvious in his voice I wondered if he was burning up inside from it. "She doesn't have an alibi. She's guilty. Now get out of my way while I arrest my suspect."

CHAPTER TWENTY-EIGHT

I fully expected my boyfriend to put Robert in his place. After all, that kind of attitude couldn't be tolerated, and I stood there in eager anticipation of the end of my cousin.

Instead, Crew frowned and motioned for his deputy to show him the image on his phone. When Robert sullenly complied, his thick mustache drooping at the edges while he glared like he was expecting the worse, Crew instead nodded and turned to the still weeping Kami.

"Good catch, deputy," he said in his gruff voice, without a hint of actual emotion behind the words. It was, however, seemingly enough to puff Robert up to the level he required to allow Crew to do his job while I gaped and wanted to kick my boyfriend in the rear for feeding my cousin's psychopathy. "Ms. Derham, can you tell me the last time you had your stun gun in your possession?" He glanced at Robert. "Before you say you discovered it was stolen?"

Wait, did they just exchange a knowing look, cops being cops over a weeping suspect? They did *not*. My boyfriend, the love of my life and the one man in the world I respected as much as my dad (don't judge me) couldn't have just had a man moment with Robert.

Oooh. Boys.

Meanwhile, I knew there was no way in Reading's recent history of murders and mayhem that Robert actually came up with this tidbit himself. This kind of snooping had Rose written all over it. But what was I to do with such information?

Blurt my own opinion, naturally.

"You could at least let her answer before you decide she's guilty." Whoa, where did that come from? Yup, I was steaming mad, you betcha, and from the arch of Crew's eyebrow he knew it and would likely make that apparent in the next second or so if I didn't stop. Which meant I couldn't stop now. "Kami, who knew you had the stun gun?"

"Everyone." She hiccupped her way through more tears. "I had a stalker guy last year and I got the stun gun for protection. He was arrested six months ago so I almost got rid of it, but you just never know in this business." She rubbed her thin arms with both hands, eyes locked on mine as if she was too afraid to look at the sheriff and deputy, like that would welcome handcuffs and more accusations.

"I think it's time you found somewhere else to be." Robert tried to use his protruding belly to bump me out of the way, hands on his belt, scowl twisting that disgusting wad of hair on his upper lip into a wriggling caterpillar desperate to escape his face.

I waited a half-second for Crew to defend me, caught him watching with narrowed eyes and felt, in that same instant of hurt and betrayal, the cold calculation of his choice. No, he wasn't siding with Robert, that much was obvious from the flash of fury in his eyes. But he wasn't above pretending, and he expected me to just take it.

We'd see about that. I wasn't playing his game.

But before I could call Crew on it, Robert whipped out a sheet of printer paper, holding it up and out of my reach with that sneer of a grin on his face that always made me want to punch him hard enough to see if I could deflate his growing gut. And now that I'd had training? Surely one solid blow would knock the air out of it like collapsing a hideously distended balloon.

"According to this list," he said, all arrogance and no substance, "you, Ms. Derham, had an affair with Henry Ostler. And, that your on-again, off-again career was due to a pregnancy." He leaned into her while her face flinched in response, a guilty look of sudden regret if ever I'd seen one. "A pregnancy you chose to end."

I wasn't interested in his opinions on abortion because, well. I just wasn't. Besides, I now suspected it wasn't the first time and that her gorging hunger in my kitchen had a demanding reason.

"Kami," I said, trying to be kind, slipping around Robert to take her hand, "how far along are you?"

She cried again, clinging to me, and this time the choking sobs were heart-wrenching. Enough so I sank down next to her and hugged her, tucking her head under my chin and rocking her while I glared at Robert and dared him to interfere without saying a word.

Smart man, though not usually something I attributed to him. He held his tongue. Crew, however, didn't. At least my boyfriend's tone was kind.

"Ms. Derham," he said, "is this true? Were you previously pregnant by Mr. Ostler? And are you again?"

Kami nodded against me, fighting for air, leaning into me and clinging on like she was going to fall through the floor and vanish if I didn't keep her here. When she finally inhaled, a long and shaking gasp, she answered. "Faith knew." She met my eyes, hers bloodshot and massive. "I was going to keep the baby this time." Kami sagged further, sobs retreating, seeming to sink inside herself now. "Henry was furious."

Crew gestured for me to let the young model go and for a moment I wanted to resist. But from his grim expression, he was going to make an issue of it and I rathered he didn't in front of Robert. I stood and let my boyfriend take her hand, guiding Kami to her feet.

"I'm going to take you to the office for a bit," he said, "and ask you more questions. Would you like a lawyer present?"

She blinked up at him, clinging to his arm as if he was her savior, not the man who planned to question her and try to wring a confession out of her. "I didn't do anything wrong."

Robert snorted but stayed quiet while Crew led Kami out of the room, following his boss with a scowl for me that was more a teen boy getting his way than a professional deputy making an arrest.

Whatever. I was done. Petunia's was calling and Crew could handle Robert from here.

Just my luck, as I walked through the front door it was to the sight of Daisy and Rose facing off in my foyer. Right, because I needed this particular confrontation tonight. Not that my bestie took Rose's side anymore these days, but she rarely spoke up against her half-sister, either, leaving me without backup and sick of the younger woman's face.

"Interfering in police business again, Fiona?" Okay, she was next. Yes, if she showed up dead everyone in town would know I did it, but it would be worth it. Right? Right?

"Look who's talking." I crossed my arms over my chest, my pug trotting to my side to sit on my feet, snorting in Rose's direction like she was waiting for the smackdown and wanted popcorn for the show. "Don't think I'm not aware that you dug up that information for Robert. So, I'm not the only one who needs to mind her own business."

Rose's eyes narrowed, her pinched face aging her well past her late twenties into wicked old witch territory. "Someone has to get this investigation right," she said, just as sullen as her boyfriend. "You and that so-called sheriff are bungling everything. It's clear that floozy model did it. If she can get an abortion, she's already committed murder."

Daisy gasped while I clenched my teeth and exhaled to the count of ten before speaking.

"Get out of my place," I said. "And never come back."

She huffed and turned to Daisy who refused to meet her eyes. "Day. *Do* something."

"*Get out.*" My bestie spun, back to her half-sister, lower lip trembling. "Just get out."

Rose's immediate reaction wasn't what I expected. In fact, it was suddenly and frighteningly chilling in its flash of interest and ugly epiphany. What two and two did she just put together? Instead of pushing her sibling, she flounced past me with a head toss while Petunia, my quiet and sweet-hearted pug, growled in her wake.

"Rose." I stopped her with her name as she opened the door. "Where did you get your hands on Faith's list?" That much I would have loved to know.

"Like I'd tell you." She slammed the door and then it was just me and Daisy and my farting pug who groaned her contentment before panting up at me like this was the most fun ever.

Wait, was Daisy crying? I had thought she

distanced herself enough from Rose since her father's funeral that my bestie wasn't so tied up in her half-sister's crap to be this choked up about telling her to get lost. I took a step in her direction, but she was already moving, heading for the kitchen, and I let her go, knowing when she was ready to talk to me she would.

Hell of a way to end my day.

CHAPTER TWENTY-NINE

Grumpy, who me? I slept badly and woke up on the wrong side of the bed to a text from Crew canceling our morning run and a string of small disasters that really weren't a big deal (ten minutes and a new hose and the washing machine was all fixed, not to mention the big dustpan and three brooms in eager hands got the pile of smashed plates off the dining room floor in short order, though the smoothie bullet explosion was my fault and took forever to scrape off Mom, the counter, the floor and every other surface in the kitchen). Thing was, you put enough small cuts together and you can bleed to death. Or something like that. I was sure that was a proverb or an old story or something, right?

Sigh. Just put me out of my misery already.

Thing was, I pondered the case as I made it through those missteps and mishaps, something irking me while I grew more and more out of sorts to the point my own mother, her red hair tucked under a kerchief to hide the remains of the smoothie she didn't have time to wash out, gestured at the kitchen door with a spoon and said, "Fiona Fleming, out!"

Well, if you feel that way about it. And I was the grumpy one. I slouched into the garden to sit by the koi pond, kicking at rocks that tumbled into the water with little plops. As I did, one of my sneakers hit a wet patch and I slipped, almost falling into the water. Petunia stared up at me as I meeped and grasped for the bench, sitting quickly to catch myself from falling. The pug sat next to me and groaned, sinking to her belly and looking up at me with those sad pug eyes while Fat Benny surfaced at the edge of the pond, thinking the pebbles were food. He wasn't called Fat Benny for nothing.

"The list." I addressed the fish as I inhaled sharply, the moment of truth striking me tied to the body memory of sliding over the wet rock. When had I slipped a few days ago? Faith's face surfaced. "Where did Rose get the list?"

Benny wriggled back under the water, but Petunia watched me with curiosity, triangle black ears perked.

"I'll tell you where," I poked the pug's nose to which she snorted. "She made it up, Petunia. Or she got her hands on something that didn't belong to her, something she had to have stolen from Faith's possessions." I settled back on the bench, grinning to myself. "Faith's notebook." Of course. Fee. What was wrong with me? The small pink notebook, the one that fell out of her purse, the one I tripped and slipped over the first time we met. The same one she seemed eager to keep private. I'd forgotten all about it until now.

Okay, so that didn't prove Rose's list was fake. She could have found the notebook and transferred the info to a document file and printed it off. But why bother? Why go to all that effort? To protect the original? No, that didn't make sense. Rose wasn't about making work for herself. She would have just handed the notebook over to Robert. More than likely, she'd been doing her own digging, came up with a possible explanation for the murder, and was using that to give Robert information. And without the real list to work from, no one would be the wiser.

I had to call Crew. Though it remained that Rose had somehow deduced that Kami was pregnant. That meant she'd been lurking around the crime scene herself. What, was she trying to turn herself into a cop? I had a herky-jerky moment of understanding that made me slightly nauseated. No, she was trying to be *me*.

Though the me of this case had been pretty absentminded. If I'd been paying closer attention, maybe I would have put the whole thing together, too. So, if I was going to be honest here, I'd been holding back, not like me. But why? Because I wasn't investigating this out of my own impetus. I was doing it because Vivian wanted me to.

Yikes. Was I really that shallow that a woman's death meant less to me than my lingering anger at Vivian French? Or was I even more shallow and getting bored with solving murders? What did that make me?

I knew one thing, though. I wasn't about to let Rose's fake list get Kami in more trouble. Not when I now knew what to look for. And froze as I half stood, heart now in my throat. Wait, I'd sent someone else looking for the list, only now giving her a second thought.

Where was Mila Martin?

I retreated to the main house and my cell phone, dialing my sheriff boyfriend and getting his voicemail. I slipped out, heading for the office, only to find Melissa there alone and clueless as to where anyone had gone.

"I just don't know." She seemed close to tears, tossing her hands as she stared at the empty blotter in front of her, blinking light on the phone telling me she had messages she hadn't retrieved yet and fully expecting her not to be sitting in that chair much longer. "No one tells me anything."

Okie doke. I headed for the lodge, my mind on Faith and that notebook, though when I ran into Alicia and inquired about Crew, she was surprised I asked.

"I haven't seen him this morning," she said. "But the fashion show is back on for tomorrow night. He didn't tell you? He cleared the crime scene."

Apparently, a lot happened between last night

and this morning he hadn't told me about. Cue grumpier mood than ever, though in all fairness he wasn't required to fill me in on his job. He was sheriff after all. Still. Grumble.

I checked in on Mom in the kitchen, still calmly managing things, and left her to her work. Right, she'd been at the lodge last night, so my worry about where she'd been prior to dinner at Petunia's had a logical explanation. Worry about Dad resurfaced and sank again as quickly while I hurried through the back hall toward the ballroom rear door, almost tripping over the giant folding sign in the middle of the corridor proclaiming the pool was closed for maintenance. I scowled at it for getting in my way and shook my head. So many distractions, so many tugs at my train of thought. No wonder I'd been fighting to keep this murder in the forefront of my mind. It had nothing to do with Vivian.

Sure, Fee. If you say so.

I stepped through the back doors into the ballroom, worried I might run into Jill and not sure what to tell her, surprised then instead to spot Grace and Mateo huddled near the wings to the catwalk. Frederick turned and offered that smarmy smile of his, reaching out to catch my hand and stop me on the way by. I resisted the urge to swat at him, hands clenched at my sides, but forced myself to pause and be polite.

"You're looking lovely, Miss Fleming." Seriously? A woman was murdered, he'd been a suspect, and he was thinking about how I looked? Me in jeans, sneakers, a t-shirt that should have been tossed months ago and a jacket that was more unisex than feminine? Come to think of it, I wasn't really trying these days, was I? Poor Crew. He had to look at this disaster of a woman I put out to the world. Resolving to make more of an effort, I smiled at Frederick and thanked him silently—if sullenly—for the reminder.

"Have you seen the sheriff?" Maybe that mention tied to the possibility of finding Crew might serve me on both ends.

Frederick's smile faded slightly but returned at full wattage. "I hear he has a suspect in custody," he said. "Noel Lewder? Or was Libby Kim the culprit?"

Fishing, was he? I ignored his question as I spotted Grace across the stage. As soon as she noticed me, she gestured for me to join her and I did, Frederick trailing after me. Let him stare at my butt, not much to see. But maybe I'd change that, for Crew's sake...? I nodded to Mateo who gave me the once over enough to make me scowl. When I turned to Grace, I noted Frederick and the handsome young designer exchanged unhappy glares. Over me? Sigh. Boys.

Grace's hand settled on my elbow and tucked me into their little circle before she spoke in a tight whisper.

"Fee, what's happening?" She glanced up as we were joined by a clearly agitated Noel. How had she gotten on stage? No one seemed surprised to see her, so maybe she'd been welcomed back into the fold. Noel, for her part, seemed happy to see me and nodded for me to answer while Frederick alone glared in her direction. Likely because she refused his advances, the cad.

"I can't tell you anything," I said.

"Kami's been arrested." Grace bit her lower lip, shook her head while Mateo inhaled sharply, clearly news to him. Noel looked equally upset, Frederick looking suddenly sick. "She couldn't have killed Faith."

Did she know something I didn't? "She doesn't have an alibi," I said. I caught myself before I spilled the rest, knowing I'd been in this spot before and accidentally released details, refusing to let my big mouth get in the way this time.

Before Grace could argue, Henry appeared, scowling at me while I stared up at him with a decision to make and regret already stirring. "Mr. Ostler," I said, "is it true Ms. Derham was pregnant with your child? And that she had an abortion to end it?"

I was expecting Henry to be angry, but I wasn't planning on Grace's reaction. She blanched, swayed and then, with a shriek of fury, launched herself at him. Henry caught her, held her off, his face not furious as I expected but full of sorrow.

"Grace—" That was all he got out when she jerked free of him and slapped him across the face so hard his head rocked back.

"You bastard!" She sobbed once, hands clenched at her sides while the others stared in a mix of horror, surprise and uncomfortable voyeurism. Yes, me included. "You knew I wanted children, you knew it was all I wanted. You said you couldn't be a father. You lied to me!" She spun then and ran off, face in her hands. Noel went after her, judgment in her expression as she glanced over her shoulder at Henry. Even Mateo and Frederick seemed put off by Henry's silence and the two drifted away, whispering to each other while I stood there next to the man I'd put in this terrible position.

He had every right to be enraged. Instead, he sighed, rubbed his face with both hands, the arrogance in him gone, only brokenhearted sadness in his eyes when they met mine. "Miss Fleming," he said, "I have no idea who told you Kami was with child of my progeny, but I can assure you, that would be quite impossible." I believed him. His hurt was too raw. "Barring a miraculous shift in physiology, there is no way in Heaven or on Earth a child's beginning could come from this body." He gestured at himself, staring after Grace with a longing that confirmed what I'd been suspecting all along. How could love go so wrong for two people who clearly adored each other that much?

"Why didn't you confront Kami when she said the babies were yours?" He could have cleared this up by calling her on the lie. But why would she lie?

He shrugged. "She chose to eliminate the first one when her blackmail attempt failed." I blinked and he offered the faintest of smiles. "She wanted money, Miss Fleming, for the abortion. When I paid it, she used that as 'proof' I was the father and tried to extort more from me." Again, no anger, just weariness. "An old story. So, I gave her some and told her to quit modeling. I, of course, made the human error of trusting her when she begged for a second chance. I have a soft spot for models, you see, damsels in distress, though there are those who would judge me for it."

Whatever, not my problem. "So, who's the actual father?" Why the elaborate ruse?

Henry finally showed a different emotion, but again not what I was expecting. He actually looked worried. "I don't know," he said. "I fear now, however, perhaps Kami was the killer after all. If Faith discovered Kami was lying about the paternity, was somehow using Kami's pregnancies against her... if she knew who the real father was, could she have committed the murder to stop Faith from revealing the truth? Too many flags point to that unfortunate young woman."

He was right. Which made me nervous. Because either I was yet again a horrible judge of character or Kami was the victim of an elaborate setup to protect the real killer.

Henry wasn't about to stay for the answer. "To be honest, I don't care anymore." He shook his head, hands outstretched in front of him, staring at them like he didn't know who they belonged to. "All I long for, Miss Fleming, is the one thing I could never give the only woman I ever loved. If I could have fathered her children, I would have. I would have given her the world."

With that, head down, he walked away, leaving me to juggle my own set of emotions, not the least of which was empathy.

CHAPTER THIRTY

I wasn't prepared to run into Jill, though I should have been. It wasn't like I didn't know she was there, lurking in the background. Okay, not really fair, but I was already struggling with feeling bad and when she appeared while I wavered on the edge of compassion for Henry Ostler, her aggressive expression and clear antagonism set me off like it wouldn't have normally.

Who was I kidding? I never did well with confrontation, friend or not.

"Why do you keep interfering?" Jill's voice vibrated with anger, her whole body trembling with it, the dark suit she wore making her look like a federal agent, maybe, but her face looking like nothing more than a petulant child playing dress-up and knowing she didn't deserve to be mistaken for more than she was.

It was a powerful insight but lost on me as I overreacted (there's a shocker).

"Why are you suddenly such a jerk?" I shot that back at her and might as well have struck her from the impact it had. Jill rocked back on her heels, her eyes wide, lips twisting into what looked like the prequel to a good sob session. What battle was she fighting with herself? Was it more than her feeling like an imposter, like she didn't belong here?

"I'm doing my job, Fee." Jill's tone hadn't softened, though she seemed more sullen than angry now.

"No," I said, jabbing her with one index finger, knowing even as I touched her, I'd gone too far but unable to stop myself. "You're not. You're doing a rent-a-cop's job while channeling Robert Carlisle and treating your friends like crap." Yup, way too far as her pupils dilated, her whole body tensing like she was ready to body slam me to the ground. But I was on a roll, whoa boy was I, and there was nothing stopping this freight train of Fleming heading for a crash into Mount Wagner. "Friends who have stood by you and supported you since day one."

She shook, a tremor as if she'd suffered her own personal earthquake, jaw jumping, broad shoulders taking on a twitch before she settled again. "Friends who've made a fool of me time and time again until I can't do my job effectively and doubt every decision I make." She looked away, licking her lips as if she regretted speaking and hated the taste of admission in her mouth. "Doubt my choice to be a cop, a job I've wanted since I was a little girl." She looked back again, met my eyes, hers totally cut off, her heart walled away while I relented inside if not outside at the fact I'd just done irreparable harm to my friend and friendship. "Thanks for that, Fee. I needed the reminder."

I grabbed her arm as she turned to leave, unwilling to just let her go. "You have nothing to doubt about yourself," I said, hasty and unprepared for this turn in the conversation. I expected a fight, not to have to defend her from her own inner demons. "You're an amazing deputy, Jill."

She shook her head, a tight motion that bobbed her ponytail across one shoulder. "No," she said, "maybe I could have been. But I made the wrong choice, coming to Reading. Listening to Crew, to you." Jill shuddered my hand from her arm, and I let her. "You know, I never thought that I'd end up agreeing with the likes of Robert. He's been getting in my head, and I've let him because I just can't seem to get past the fact I've failed as a cop. So maybe it was meant to be, that I ended up here. I needed the wake-up call, that the dream I had, this job," she looked down at her hands as she raised them in front of her, clenching them into fists, "is better than me."

God, what had Robert been saying to her? "Jill." I inhaled, scrambled for words. But I was too late, wasn't I? She'd been fighting this battle for a while now and I'd failed to see it. Failed her, ultimately.

"I knew it when you were almost shot," she said,

voice now low and dull, empty of hope. "When I botched the Black Mountain investigation, when you solved it before I could, almost died twice because I wasn't up to the job." She met my gaze one last time, hers devoid of the energetic and passionate woman I'd called my friend, only the shell of her remaining. "Maybe I should be grateful I found out before I was too old, too jaded and broken by the job, that I need to move on. But I'm not, Fee. I'll never be grateful. I hate it here." Those fists tightened further, her whole expression altering to utter fury, body shaking once more while I gaped and wished there was something I could do or say. "*Hate* it. I'm quitting, leaving Reading. And I'll regret coming here for the rest of my life."

She spun and stomped away, leaving me to watch her go with my heart in my shoes and my frustration levels at an all-time high. There was nothing to be done, with Crew absent and still not answering his phone. I did take a perfunctory look around for Mila but came up empty, so I headed for my car, texting as I walked, the inevitable trip over my own foot making me pay more attention. Seriously, I knew better. I paused to finish, wondering where Crew had gone but determined to put it out of my mind.

The rest of the day passed without a whisper from him, and I grew increasingly worried, angry and—you guessed it—frustrated by the entire situation. Why invite me into the investigation if he was going to ignore me? Of course, then I spun into concern he was hurt, or the killer had somehow incapacitated him winding toward the fact he really didn't care and was trying to placate me by offering to allow me access to what he knew.

Whew. When I chose to, I could really make myself crazy.

It was late, after 11PM as I huddled on my couch with my pug in my lap, scowling at my TV while it tried its hardest to entertain and distract me, failing miserably. I had finally decided to just go to bed after several rounds of fighting off the urge to go looking for Crew when a new message popped up and turned me around the way I'd come.

I found the list. It had to be from Mila. How did she get my phone number? *And I know who the real killer is.*

Holy crap. *Where are you?* I looked up from my screen, already on my feet, heading for the stairs, Petunia whining as I left her behind.

Backstage, she sent.

One more drive up the mountain? Okie doke.

I slipped in the rear door of the lodge to avoid questions. Fine, to avoid Jill and Matt. I didn't want to stir that particular pot any further. Instead, I used the entrance by the ski lift, the doors further down locked tight from the outside, something I knew from personal experience. Yeah, I really didn't want to think about almost dying in a snowstorm on Valentine's Day right about now, not when the thought struck me as I entered the dark back hall and let myself into the quiet staging area that there was a distinct possibility the text message I'd received hadn't come from Mila.

That stopped me in my tracks and made my heart speed up. Wow, Fee, way to just trust and act like some kind of first-timer. I knew better than to throw myself into danger like this and anticipated Crew's disapproving scowl after he hugged me within an inch of my life.

I hesitated and considered retreating, noting the backstage area screen off by towering black velvet curtains was silent, dark, still. Yeah, this really was a terrible idea.

"Mila?" That came out in a squeaking whisper, met by silence. I caught myself trembling, feet frozen to the floor, ears straining for any sign I wasn't alone. Nothing, save for the muffled sounds coming from the lobby outside the main doors what felt like miles away and the hum of air conditioning overhead.

Well, I was here, and Crew wasn't and I could just call Jill and Matt for help if something happened, right? Sure thing, Fee, you just keep telling your ridiculous red head that if it makes you feel better. I shook off the internal talk and forced a step forward. I'd just find Mila, get the list and catch the murderer and everything would be fine.

By the time I'd finished searching the backstage area my fear had turned to annoyance at my own fears. There was no one there, not a soul, not even Mila. Frustration and anxiety were not my favorite mix of emotions and so when I finally sorted out that I'd come on a wild goose chase, I was vexed enough I paused to kick at a rack of clothes just to vent some of my pique.

I glanced down as I did, and noticed a small, pink notebook next to my foot. No way I was this lucky...? I bent, retrieved it, flipped it open to the last page. And gasped as I realized I now knew who the killer was, too.

Two things happened in that instant, both of which fed into each other in a slow-motion unfolding of fresh fear I shouldn't have let slip. First was the reveal of the unconscious form of Mila Martin, once hidden by that very rack of clothing, now exposed as I looked up from the book, her pale face turned toward me. That would have been bad enough, thanks, but life wasn't done with me.

No, in the instant it took me to understand what I was seeing, I felt something cold press to the base of my neck just as a sharp jolt of electricity raced through me and brought me to my knees.

CHAPTER THIRTY-ONE

My eyes fluttered open, head aching, heart skipping a bit before it settled down into a more natural rhythm while I did my best to make sense of the foggy surfacing memories floating around in my sore noggin. The acutely acrid scent of chlorine assaulted my nose, warm, moist air making me choke a little. I tried to focus, something hard and damp under my cheek, my hand slipping over what felt like tile as I blinked at the edge of concrete rimming an impossibly blue pool of water.

I registered where I was as a shadow passed over me, stepping across my legs, his face appearing in my vision and speeding my heart rate as I fought to regain control of my spasming limbs. I'd had stun gun training, thanks to Dad. I'd even had one tested on me for a half-second, so I'd know what it felt like, and it wasn't something I'd wanted to repeat. To render me unconscious? My attacker had to have held the gun to me forever.

Bastard.

Though I shouldn't have expected much from Frederick Newmark. It was him, after all, who appeared in my wavering sight, who scowled at me, then over my shoulder as if assessing what he was going to do next. I attempted a gurgled swear at him but all that came out was a grunt. His eyes fixed on me, beads of sweat standing out on his upper lip. Even in my disoriented state, I could tell he was in pure panic mode.

The talk outside his room? I'd briefly thought it had been an act, meant to distract and deflect me, to make me think he was just that clueless. But as I stared in his eyes, I realized it wasn't. The man was an idiot, gaze vacant of reason or even two crumbs of a plan to rub together and that terrified me.

Now, I'd dealt with cold-blooded killers, vengeful sweethearts and even accidental murderers, but I'd never had to face someone with this level of panic in their face, worn in their manner, and I knew in that instant Frederick was the most dangerous murderer I'd ever confronted. Not because he was brilliant or psychotic or even talented. But because he was an utter idiot and so very afraid of getting caught.

I inhaled, trying to fill my lungs for another shot at speaking, as he disappeared from view. I heard him grunt himself, felt him stumble over my foot and watched, flinching, as he fell next to me, the still unconscious Mila in his arms. Her head tumbled to one side, long hair hanging over the edge of the pool while he panted his desperate need to finish whatever nefarious plan he had etched into his aging but still handsome face.

"Stop." I managed to whisper that one word, hand wriggling as I fought to control it, to grab for Mila. He slapped me away, suddenly pinched, desperate.

"You have to understand I can't stop now." So matter of fact despite his fear, so utterly devoid of reason. "She had the list." He gestured at Mila, met my eyes again, his wild around the edges. "She saw what Faith knew. And so did you, Ms. Fleming. That means you both have to die like that conniving little bitch did."

I shook my head, or tried to, forcing myself to remember what I'd read. "Baby," I said. Something about Kami's babies.

"Exactly." He ran one shaking hand over his perspiring face, staring down at it a moment before wiping it clean on his pants. Apparently, he didn't know DNA evidence was a problem for him at this point, but if he succeeded in what I now feared he had in mind, the water might wash away anything Crew could use to solve my murder.

Oh. My. God. He was going to drown me in the pool and there was nothing I could do about it. My own panic woke in a shrieking demon of absolute denial, giving me enough power to roll over onto my back as my mind begged my body to get up and run. The terror of almost drowning last August lingered like no other nightmare, if I was going to be honest about it, and oddly, in that moment, I had a brief and horrible instant of childlike panic, hearing a young boy's voice screaming my name. But there was no time to ponder the memory or whatever it was that surfaced, not when Frederick's stare turned from freaked out to determined and I recalled the closed for maintenance sign I'd almost tripped over in the back hallway. Any chance of rescue was dashed. No one would be coming. I was on my own.

No, not quite. I had Mila. But she was out cold still, pale and silent in the faintly green-tinted light of the pool lights, the only illumination in the room. For all I knew, she was already dead.

Frederick, meanwhile, had caught his breath, glaring down at Mila like this was her fault. "I tried to make it look like suicide, but I botched it." Was that self-recrimination? A lifetime of it creeping up to make him doubt himself? "I botched everything." He met my eyes again, and this time he looked needy, as if he wanted me to absolve him of his crimes even my own pending death perimortem. "It was Kami's idea, the pregnancies. To trap Henry. Easy money, she said. How was I to know Henry was sterile?" He was shaking now, sweating all over again, droplets falling on Mila's white blouse, leaving tiny pinpoints of slowly expanding dark spots. Fascinating where my mind went to hide when death loomed. I'd always planned to ponder this response I typically had to impending mortality, but never got around to it, hoping each time I almost died at the hands of a murderer would be my last.

"Don't have to." I meant to say he didn't have to kill me. Us. Correction, Mila included. Frederick seemed to think I meant something else because he shook his head, scowling at the silent pool water, the lights on the bottom casting their sickeningly green glow over everything.

"I did have to," he said. "I was out of options. Henry was going to fire me. The allegations of that girl, well." He sniffed like she'd offended him. "She wanted it. How was that my fault? I had no idea she was sixteen." Again the appeal to me to justify his acts. "She said she was twenty-one. Was I supposed to ask for ID?"

Just ew, dude.

"I have no prospects." Frederick's voice dropped to a dull acceptance, his face creasing with anger then nothing at all as it went slack. "I know that. I'm fully aware I'm a washed-up almost was. Henry was my only connection to the industry, the only one willing to consider my designs. Faith offered to help, was stealing from Mateo to share with me. I hooked her up with my dealer, even." He trembled violently a moment. "Only to turn around and tell me she wanted money from me, that Mateo found out and was going to expose her. That she'd ruin me." Frederick was a mess, clearly so freaking lost inside his own narcissism he thought he could get away with such things in a closed and close-knit community. "Henry was going to cut me loose. Served him right. Except it didn't work, did it?" He hit the floor suddenly with one fist before nursing the hurt against his chest with a shocked expression. "It didn't work. Kami promised. Then she killed our baby."

Oh, wow. Just holy Hannah in a handbasket. "Sorry." I really was. He seemed genuinely damaged by it, not to mention all over the place. What worried him more, losing his potential child or Mateo bringing the thefts to Henry?

Must have been the stunning that made me think he was actually a real person. He jerked like I'd hit him and scowled. "We could have figured something else out," he snapped. "But she decided to double-cross me and cut me out entirely. Had the abortion on Henry's dime and was going to leverage that information to get him to pay her off. She refused to talk to me at all. So, when Faith came to me with the Mateo deal, I took it. Of course, I took it."

Okies, you heartless jerk.

"Then that little sneak, Faith, found out about Kami when the two fought over that piece of crap Mateo like they always did." Frederick started to shake again, this time his anger so clear, so visible on his face, in his body, I feared for Mila who lay in his grasp. Just his touch alone must have felt like an assault with that much hate running through him. Never mind his intent to shove her in the pool. "Did she go to Kami, though? No, she came to me. Showed me the DNA test Kami had done proving it was mine. She was going to tell Henry." Another swipe at his sweaty face, but not an ounce of fear remaining, only that chilling expression of vile vitriol. "She made a deal with me. Turned me against the other models. I can't believe I went along with it." He coughed a laugh. "She was clever, I'll give her that. I was the one who set up Noel, for Faith. Grace was going to hire Noel as her headliner. Faith couldn't handle that. I spiked Noel's drink." He choked a moment. "And I was the one who convinced Grace to abandon Henry. The least I could do." That explained a lot. I felt my body shudder, tingling in my extremities making me gasp, though my mind had cleared further, my vision and I knew if I could just keep Frederick talking a few more minutes I might stand a chance.

Might.

"Kami." I felt my mouth respond and did my best to fake continuing incapacitation. "Custody. Talking." Maybe I could get him to run and leave us.

Yeah, apparently my head wasn't as straight as I thought because my plan had the opposite effect. Frederick freaked, panic returning, squeaking out a mouse-like squeal of terror, huge eyes meeting mine. "I know," he said. "What am I going to do?"

CHAPTER THIRTY-TWO

Um, crazy dude was asking me? I rolled back over with a lurching shove. "Turn yourself in."

He was almost too far gone, staring, shivering. "I can't. When I saw Faith that night she came to me, wanted me to humiliate Kami, tell Henry the baby was mine. Both babies." He looked down at Mila then back at me as if he couldn't figure out where he was suddenly or what he was doing there. "I refused. I knew if I turned on Kami, she'd be the one to out me to Henry. And I had Henry convince to keep me on. But if I didn't, Faith was going to ruin me, already planned to tell the cops about the drugs, that she was dealing because of me. I knew she'd win." He seemed so lost, so deplorably confused, I almost felt sorry for the man he might have been once upon a time. "I'd taken Kami's stun gun a week ago when we had a fight. She'd threatened me with it, and I wanted it out of her hands." Did Kami know he'd taken it? Why hadn't she said anything? Didn't matter now, but I'd be asking her if I didn't die of drowning in the next few minutes. Just keep him talking, Fee. "Faith turned her back on me, the little minx." There was the anger all over again. "So, I stunned her." One more flash of shock, like he had no idea how his life had come to this moment. "I wasn't intending to kill her. I just wanted to stop her. But I think I might have lost my mind. She was in that dress, Mateo's dress, complaining about it, like always. We were alone and the ladder was beside me and I just... I had to humiliate her as she'd been humiliating me all this time."

Fear and belittling, two powerful murder motivations. Not to mention money, drugs, ego. Yup, from where I was lying, fighting for control of my body, Faith didn't stand a chance.

"List," I said, flexing my thighs, my calves, knowing I was almost okay. So close.

He glared suddenly at Mila. "I was backstage hunting for it when I heard that ridiculous deputy had produced a fake." Not that I needed validation, but yeah. Validation. Robert was in so much trouble. "Your little friend here had the book, was already reading it, called me out when she saw me. I had to stun her." He shook his head. "I didn't want to, but I had no choice. And she'd already texted you, so, I had to wait for you, too." He swallowed hard. "I didn't think she'd told you anything, but I had to know for sure. She threw the book!" Frederick sat up suddenly, furious. "She threw it and then I stunned her and stunned her and stunned her." He twitched, hands clenching in front of him. "I think she's already dead."

I was pretty sure of it. After all, she hadn't even twitched, and he'd attacked her long before me. So hard to tell in the low light, the dark circles under her eyes looking cadaverous. I felt a wave of sympathy and horror for her, guilt beating me hard while I fought tears. My fault. I'd sent her chasing the list when I should have had Crew make sure she was somewhere she wouldn't be able to harm herself or others.

Guilt was for later. Right now, I had to deal with this man who stumbled from disaster to disaster without knowing what he was doing, without feeling the empathy for him I might have in another circumstance since he reminded me so much of myself at times.

"Killing us won't help," I said, finally relenting and getting a full sentence out even if it meant alerting him to the fact I was wide awake and physically recovered. Though that was a guess since I hadn't had the chance to properly test my body against gravity. "Kami will tell Crew everything. You'll be caught, Frederick. Turn yourself in and let us go and you might get leniency."

Frederick stared at me a long moment before reaching for his right front pocket. The stun gun was small, innocuous but imminently threatening as he clicked it on, the spark jumping in a rattling warning while his blank expression told me I'd gone too far.

"I'll take my chances," he said.

I had to act and gathered myself to lunge for him just as Mila's eyes snapped open and she sat up. Frederick stared at her in gaping shock, the stun gun falling from his hand. I made my move, scrambling forward for it, my body still slow, too slow it felt like, heart hammering in response to the terror I let out at last. Frederick was faster, his hand finding the gun again, shoving it against Mila's neck. The pair struggled a moment while I threw myself into him to stop him but too late. The rattle of the spark woke, and Mila jerked, tumbling backward out of his arms and into the water.

The world took on super focus as my heart stopped. Not me drowning, but someone I knew and felt responsible for, enough of a kick in the pants I literally snapped into hyper-awareness. Again, I heard the boy's voice calling my name, felt a jerking distortion as if time had suddenly shifted out of my control, memory and reality crossing paths in a heart-stopping layered image of a blonde child sinking underwater superimposed over Mila's disappearing form.

I lunged at Frederick as I snapped back to the here and now, the boy's scream gone, Jill's voice in my head instead. *Fee, block!* Her commands moved my hands to stop the forward motion of the stun gun in his hand, knocking it away, driving the other into his exposed throat.

I have no idea where she came from or why she was there, but as the door swung open and Jill's startled face appeared, I screamed Mila's name in the same instant my blow struck Frederick's Adam's apple. He fell backward, clutching at his neck while I grasped for the stun gun and drove it into his chest, pressing the button and holding it down, feeling a hysterical giggle emerging, unable to stop it from rising like bubbles from the pool to the sound of Jill diving into the water.

I held him down, his body twitching and writhing beneath me, watching his face turn beet red, my peripheral mind hearing splashing, Jill calling my name, hands on my shoulders jerking me back and away from Frederick who, despite being free of the stun gun, continued to twitch and moan. I sobbed once, unable to stop the exhalation of emotion, hugging Jill tight while she crouched next to me, feeling someone else embrace me on the other side, the pair of wet arms squeezing while Mila's voice whispered my name in my ear.

"My sheroes," I whispered and broke down into tears.

CHAPTER THIRTY-THREE

Crew's arms felt about the best they ever had as he held me against him, chin on the top of my head, the familiar scent of him filling me with more comfort than I think he'd ever understand. Jill stood close by, still dripping, reporting to the FBI agent my boyfriend brought in to take over the investigation. Not that he didn't want to handle it, but with the cross-state crimes tied to the murders, he deemed it smart and from the way his old partner, Liz Michaud, greeted him when she arrived with her new sidekick, she agreed.

Funny, she'd always been a bit cold to me, standoffish when we'd met. This time she smiled warmly and hugged me despite the wet the other two women had transferred to me, before letting me go.

"You're okay, Fee?" So, we were on a first name (and nickname) basis? Awesome.

"Thanks, Liz," I said, settling into Crew's arms. He hugged me enthusiastically and I remained there while the paramedics checked over Mila, Liz's partner standing over the young woman, though to protect her or to protect others from her I wasn't sure.

"I had an interaction with Ms. Fleming." Jill sounded stilted like she didn't know how to address Liz, but the FBI agent just accepted and wrote down what the deputy (was she still?) told her. "I regretted what was said and I phoned her to apologize. I was backstage at the time, doing a sweep, and heard her phone ring." Jill glanced my way, cheeks pink. She was going to say she was sorry? I nodded to her, and she nodded back as she went on. "I found it and knew something wasn't right, so I went looking for her. Knowing she has a nose for getting herself into trouble and finding killers and bodies at the same time." Jill was grinning now, so all was forgiven. And frankly, I was more than happy about that fact. We'd work out our fight, move on. Maybe I could talk her out of quitting and leaving Reading, shedding her doubts about herself in the process. We'd see. But from the way she was relaxing, filling in more details with her professional and solid manner in full swing, I was pretty sure she wasn't on the brink like she had been earlier. Hope. I'd take it.

"Jill's a hero," I said, loud enough for Liz to hear, for everyone to hear, actually. Water carried sound better than I expected. I wasn't planning on the stares or her glancing around, blushing again. Instead of backtracking, I decided to use it to my full advantage—and hers. "I'd be dead without her and so would Mila."

The young woman nodded enthusiastically, her wide-eyed stare riveted on my deputy friend, and I winced as I realized she'd managed to transfer the damaged Mila's attention from me to her own wide shoulders.

Jill finished with a nod to Liz and joined me and Crew, her head down but without any remaining antagonism toward either of us. "I was an idiot." She choked that out, not looking at me, not looking at her boss. "I'm sorry. I'm rethinking everything." Her expression turned to a scowl as Robert entered the pool area, Rose beside him, the arrogance in both of them making me want to test the stun gun's range. "I can't believe I listened." Jill finally looked up and met Crew's calm blue eyes. "If I haven't burned my bridges, Boss, I'd love to stay on."

He nodded instantly, letting me go long enough to shake her hand. "There's no one else I'd rather have at my back, Wagner." He actually sounded choked up, the arm still around me tightening and I grinned at both of them while they exchanged a firm clasp of each other's forearms.

"Seriously, just hug it out." I winked at my boyfriend who coughed a laugh, Jill snorting before punching Crew in the shoulder.

"Getting into more than you can handle again,

were you, Fanny?" Robert had terrible timing. I wasn't in the mood—or any kind of shape—to retort, but I needn't have bothered. Jill turned and put herself physically between him and me, hands on her hips, still dressed in her suit only now she looked freaking impressive.

"As usual," she said, "Fee led us right to the killer." She sniffed, looking him up and down, not even sparing the scowling Rose a look. "Unlike you, leading us on a false trail with fake evidence."

Crew twitched and I glanced at him, caught the edge of his smile he smothered instantly, but I could tell from the twinkle in his eyes he was delighted to have Jill back and so was I.

Robert spluttered, floored, but Rose wasn't anywhere near as incompetent as her boyfriend. If anything, she was the more dangerous, as far as I was concerned, his dark and nasty hidden self notwithstanding. The clever and despicable woman at his side spoke up before he could formulate whatever excuse his feeble brain was trying to assemble.

"At least Robert is at work, doing his best," she said. "Unlike some of the sheriff's department."

Jill jerked, her whole body twitching and I had a feeling this wasn't going to end well. The thing was, it was likely Rose had something to do with the fact Jill took this rent-a-cop job in the first place, so it had to feel like a blow to the gut to hear such words in public from Robert's girlfriend. What had the pair told her? Were they pretending to be her friend, to have her back? Surely, she hadn't fallen for that from them. I wanted to defend her, but this was Jill's issue to deal with.

"Honestly, Jill," Rose said, twisting the knife, "if you had been dedicated to your duties as a deputy, maybe you could have figured out who killed that poor model without Fiona almost drowning." She made a face in my direction. "Again." Like that was a tired and boring option for me to choose.

Okay, so maybe I wasn't going to leave this to Jill because Rose had involved me, right? Crew's arms around me held me, though, and I silently fumed while the blonde deputy seemed to pull herself together.

Thing was, Jill never got the chance to respond. Mila appeared out of nowhere—or, rather, moved fast enough to evade her FBI guard—and leaped on Rose with a screech of fury. "HOW DARE YOU?" Something chattered, the sizzling spark of the stun gun hitting the female half of Rosebert in the neck and making her teeth rattle together. Rose hit the deck with a gurgling gasp, Mila on top of her, the still-active gun held firmly against her throat, while the FBI agent struggled to pull the wiry and determined crazy woman off her victim.

My first reaction should have been to leap to Rose's rescue, right? So should Crew's. Jill's. But it was a full three seconds before I felt my boyfriend's arms relax as if to release me, before Jill unwound like she was going to act. Only Robert made an effort, but his was weak and ineffectual.

Mila finally ended her attack, but only when the tall, strong agent lifted her bodily, kicking and screaming, from the prone form of Rose, the stun gun she'd stolen from the evidence bag left far too close to her falling to the pool deck with a clatter. She settled as soon as she was free, beaming at Jill who, shaken but composed, nodded back.

Robert, meanwhile, cradled Rose's head in his lap while the paramedics hurried toward him. He jabbed a finger at Mila in the grasp of the suit. "You'll pay for that!" Wow, I was really scared for her. He meant it. Snort.

Oh, Fee. Shame.

"You're welcome, Deputy Wagner." Mila sounded positively blissful. The agent hurriedly carried her from the area, out the doors, but she could be heard long after the door swung shut behind her. "I'll see you again soon!"

Yikes. I looked up at Crew who looked down at me and I swear I saw his lips twitch into a grin. A fast check on Jill met the same look, the exact same smirk.

So, my love and my friend shared an evil streak? The same one that made me want to giggle hysterically all over again? I'd take it.

CHAPTER THIRTY-FOUR

The good thing about being hit with a stun gun was the recovery. Yes, I felt like crap for about twelve hours, shaken and my muscles aching and sore, but unlike almost drowning and going through pneumonia or being hit on the head and waiting out a concussion, I was pretty much back to normal after a solid night's sleep.

I checked my email in bed, laptop on my knees, pug at my side, and was surprised to find one from Alice Moore. *Thanks for letting me borrow your dad*, she sent. Huh. Whatever that meant. *Let's have coffee when I get home and I'll tell you all about it.*

She had a date.

The hoped-for message from Pamela Shard was nowhere to be found, neither by phone or by text or email either. She was clearly avoiding me and until I figured out the Patterson thing, I guess this was going to be a habit. Not that I liked it, or the fact that when I tried to call Alicia, she sent me to voicemail. Not this again?

Jill's appearance with coffee and a grin was at least welcome. Daisy joined us, and I got to spend a fun hour or so giggling with the girls over boys and girly things, something I never expected from Jill. Nice to know our relationship was no longer rocky. When she rose to leave and I contemplated getting up at last, Jill hugged me.

"It's going to be okay, right?" She seemed suddenly lost, small, hurting.

"Stick it out," I said. "Trust Crew. Robert's days are numbered."

I didn't mean murder, but, well. If his body showed up? I'd be suspect #1.

Crew's explanation he'd been digging into Malcolm Murray in search of the means to help Libby/Eve satisfied my curiosity about where he'd been, and my father's return—refusing to tell me anything while hugging me and chastising me in his deep, graveled voice about almost dying again—shut down any further interrogations I could have offered him.

For now. There was a lot I had to ask my dad about, and he wasn't going to like any of it.

I was sad to find that Grace had checked out without saying goodbye, Libby, too, though I was pretty sure the sight of the FBI in my driveway when

I got home, Liz and her partner exiting without stopping to talk meant they were hopefully taking care of the situation.

I found myself at Vivian's door the next morning, Mom and Daisy sending me off for a free day to catch my breath. Like that was going to happen. Turned out, as I was welcomed into the inner sanctum my desire to talk to Grace personally was actually possible. She'd come to stay with the Queen of Wheat. Why she hadn't in the first place I wasn't sure, but it surely had something to do with the state of Vivian's family.

Both Grace and Libby were there, the young woman looking harried and not herself, though perhaps she was much more herself now than she'd ever been, finally able to show her fear. I hoped things went well for her from here, that the FBI could protect her, but I honestly wasn't holding my breath. Not until I had a chance to talk to a certain Irishman.

I was ushered in by a quiet maid who closed the doors to the large sitting room behind me, no sign of Clara or Martha. Only Vivian stood in front of one of the tall windows, the sunlight creating her in silhouette, slim, perfectly dressed, almost statue-like in her stillness.

Grace, on the other hand, stood and hurried to me, hugging me to her in a tight embrace. "Are you all right?"

"I'm fine," I said, patting her back before letting her go. She examined me just in case, fingers brushing over the red mark left behind on my collarbone by the stun gun.

"We were so worried." She turned and smiled sadly at Libby who had stood to join us, and her assistant nodded in response. Gone was her guarded nature, her Goth-like attempt to hide who she was. Eve O'Shea instead stared back at me, light eye makeup and her hair in soft waves around her feeling much more authentic.

"I can't believe Frederick was behind this." She squeezed my hand. "I didn't think he had it in him."

"Are *you* all right?" I squeezed back. "I told Crew about your situation. He and his old partner in the FBI want to discuss your options." Did Liz miss her after all?

Eve shrugged and sighed. "I won't testify against my family, Fee. That's what the FBI requires if they are going to help me."

"We'll see," I said. "Just meet with them?"

She finally agreed while Vivian quietly joined us.

"The fashion show is moving ahead, if delayed." She sounded all business.

Grace hugged her, too. "Thanks to you, my dear, and your continuing support." She smiled at Vivian fondly before blushing a little. "I spoke to Henry. We're working together again, if on a trial basis." Working, as in work-work or working as in...? She inhaled quickly and answered my unspoken question. "He's explained everything, and I, in turn. We're attempting to make amends to each other. To combine our efforts instead of working against each other." She sounded very happy about that, though Vivian showed no signs of agreeing and Eve looked slightly concerned.

I, for one, was rooting for love, thanks.

"I've decided Kami needs to move on." She was rather firm about that. I hardly blamed her. "And I've asked Noel to join my company. I feel it was a healthy move, for both of us." Maybe Grace could do something to help the once ousted model recover herself. I was all for it.

Vivian showed me out. I paused at the door, wanting to ask her about her aunt and grandmother, about the now achingly clear memory I'd been trying to suppress since Mila almost drowned. The boy in the water, screaming my name. Was that Victor? Why couldn't I remember?

Instead of opening that wound, I reached for her hand like Eve had for mine and squeezed her fingers ever so slightly. When she returned the touch, I took that as a sign she was willing to move ahead if I was.

"You were really brave to give up everything for your family, Vivian." I had no qualms saying it, either. "It couldn't have been easy."

She seemed momentarily floored by my words but recovered quickly. "This wasn't the life I wanted," she said, voice low, trembling ever so slightly. "But it's the one I have, so I'm making the most of it." She glanced at the sitting-room door. "Friends like Grace make it more bearable, though being in touch with what I lost isn't easy, I admit it."

Friends like Grace. I nodded, released her hand,

only to feel her squeeze one more time while the possibility she was reaching for more than just physical touch made me pause and, as she had, return the favor. I stared at her a long moment, Vivian looking back, not knowing what to say or really to feel. We weren't friends. Yet. But was that on the horizon after all?

"I need allies," Vivian finally said, keeping her voice down, but this time with an intensity that made me pay close attention. "Fee, there are things happening in Reading that are making me uncomfortable." She cleared her throat, a delicate sound, the closest to vulnerable I'd ever seen her. "I used to be able to count on you." Wow, where did that come from? Even she seemed surprised by the statement and yet again I thought of the drowning boy, considered bringing up what I was beginning to remember, decided against it as she went on. "I know you have this town's best interest at heart. Can I call on you when the time comes?" Her icy eyes no longer seemed cold, but intent, focused. "And will you trust me to do what's right, what's necessary?"

Hadn't I told myself I'd be looking for a way to make Marie Patterson sit up and take notice? I didn't even hesitate, though just a week ago I might have. "Whatever you need," I said.

Vivian's relief came through in her touch, in her eyes and she nodded before opening the door and letting me go.

As I drove away, chest tight with worry, I couldn't help but wonder just what I'd agreed to but positive I was going to find out sooner rather than later. And that it likely had something to do with the Pattersons. While Victor's death clearly lingered inside me, the reminder of his loss so long ago likely the reason memories were surfacing, it had nothing to do with my present circumstance. Didn't I have enough to keep me occupied without digging into an accident I clearly chose to forget?

No more mysteries. The proverbial inn was full.

Besides, the ones I had at my disposal deserved my full attention. I didn't get to ponder the treasure, Siobhan Doyle or the Patterson family's part in whatever Vivian had cooking because my phone pinged, and a check of the incoming text message made my heart clench.

Need to see you, Malcolm sent. *Now.*

I made it past his bullies without a fight, half-expecting one despite the fact he'd asked me to come. One never really knew when it came to Malcolm. And he was drunk, that much was apparent, in his slouched position next to a tumbler and a near-empty bottle of what looked like Scotch. He sat alone at a table in the corner of his silent establishment, windows shuttered, lights low, Malcom rattling ice in the bottom of his glass before setting it down with a thud.

He looked up as I entered, staring me down while he toyed with his empty drink, pouring another before I could even come to a halt next to him. I stood, hands tucked awkwardly in my pockets, throat aching with more than the injury I'd sustained from

Frederick, while Malcolm spoke like I'd asked him the question I'd been thinking for days.

"The woman I love is lost." He was almost unintelligible, and it took me a moment to make out what he said in his thick Irish accent. When I finally understood the string of words, I gasped, sinking down next to him, my worry about Siobhan clearly justified.

"She's dead?" How horrible. Was fate really so cruel?

But he shook his head, taking a deep drink of the fresh glass, the last drops of amber liquid in the bottle next to him likely to follow in short order. "Oh, no, lass, that would be too easy, wouldn't it, then?" He stared at the Scotch in his glass a long moment. "Far too easy. And a mercy, something we don't deserve, it seems. None for me or her in this life, God unwilling."

I leaned in and grasped his wrist, his free hand cold under mine. "What happened?"

"A stroke." He shook slightly, tears forming in his normally cold and calculating eyes. I saw his main bully lean toward him (I had to actually find out this guy's name at some point, like we were on a first-name basis), standing behind him in protective, sorrowful guardianship and realized even men like Malcolm Murray knew love, connection, family. "Took her mind, it did, just like that." He looked up then, weary and old, the energy gone out of him, the frightening man I half-liked, half-feared gone and replaced with someone I didn't understand but could feel compassion for. "We had no time, darling Fee. No chance, we two. I knew better, knew a man like me couldn't ever have the happiness she brought me, not for long. And I was right."

Fear woke in me, that he'd fall into darkness. Malcolm always seemed to have this bright shininess to him, softening the edges of his wicked ways. I really did like him, admired him, even. Part of me wished I'd had more of a chance to get to know him up to now and was grateful for the role he'd played in my life in the past. But at this moment, I honestly feared he might get lost in the hurt that played across his face. Without hope, what could a man like him become?

But no, I knew as I observed him drink again, sagging once more, he was a far better soul than he gave himself credit for. Not the darkness for this one, but emptiness, yes. He was lost, long gone, and would likely end up alone and powerless in short order.

"I'm so sorry." For a lot of things. I found I could barely speak, choking up over the layers of regret I felt for him.

Malcolm leaned in slowly, like it took effort, one hand rising to stroke my cheek in the most tender touch I'd ever felt, his own wet with tears. "Find out what happened to my Fiona. Please, dear lassie, if you can. Save an old man from himself and find my daughter."

I wanted to cry, to hug him, but he was leaning back again, sighing, snapping his fingers. Another of his boys hurried forward with a fresh bottle and I knew I wouldn't have much more time with him coherent let alone upright.

"I need to know what happened." I grasped for his hand again, but he didn't let me hold on, shaking his head.

"It means uncomfortable truths. About John. About me and Siobhan. About my daughter." He met my eyes again. "But I deserve to know. My darling deserves to know, too."

"Malcolm, I can't help you if you won't tell me what to look for." He had to understand that.

He reached into his breast pocket, fumbling a few times and I knew he was far drunker than he appeared. When he finally fished out the piece of paper, I took it from him before he could drop it in his glass by accident. *Fiona Doyle* was written across it, with a date, *June 14th*, but no year. I looked up as he nodded, jabbing a finger at the scrap of a note.

"Everything you need to know is right there," he said, eyes suddenly intense and fixed on me. "Including how *you* came to be."

Me? I almost squeaked in surprise but didn't get to talk about it further. Bully (that name would have to do) stepped toward me as if on some sort of silent cue and helped me physically to my feet. And by helped me I mean he pulled me up, gently but with firm assurance I wasn't going to win if I fought him.

"Malcolm." I tugged hard enough I won the battle, if not the war, and felt Bully relent a moment. "We need to talk about Eve O'Shea."

He knew exactly what I meant, didn't say a word.

"She just wants to live in peace." I held my breath, knowing I was toeing a line. We'd had only personalish interactions to this point, though he'd helped me catch some stray thieves in the past. But that had been in his interest. This? This was crossing paths with what amounted to family.

I was surprised when he finally spoke. "You find her," he said, "and I've never heard of Eve O'Shea."

Impossible to miss the giant twitch in the massive hand of the man who held me still. And then we were moving, him leading me to the door, gently depositing me outside. I stared up at him, his dark eyes, his tight haircut, thick neck, lips tight in a frown of worry.

"Miss Fleming," he spoke in a soft tenor, "please. They'll kill him if he goes against the family." With that, he softly closed the door.

I found myself outside on the sidewalk in the chill air, hugging my coat around me, clutching Fiona's name in my hand and holding Malcolm's life in my grasp. Not surprisingly then I felt cold inside that had nothing to do with the weather.

I drove home, stunned, terrified to go digging, anxious about Malcolm's safety despite myself—the man was a criminal who had made his choices—but knowing I had to. As I passed Watters Antiques, I remembered Oliver Watters mentioned knowing something about Dad and Malcolm and, determined to give the broken man at the bar and his true love closure if I could, no matter what it meant for my father, I checked the closed sign and agreed to myself I'd be calling on him in the morning.

I should have gone right home. But I couldn't bring myself to resume life as usual. Nor could I force myself to do an internet search of her name and that date just yet. Instead, I drove, out of Reading, into the mountains, following the highway, ignoring my phone and just putting distance under my tires.

It was a long and weary day of me pulling over to cry and argue with myself. I loved my dad and my mom. I couldn't do anything to hurt them. But if I could help Malcolm… and if this was, indeed, connected to me, didn't I owe it to him, to Siobhan and to myself to find out what was going on? I had an odd need then to unload this on Vivian French of all people and laughed at myself at last. I guess she was becoming a friend after all, if ours was one of the weirdest friendships ever.

Would she talk to me about Victor? I wanted to know about him, suddenly, with an ache that left me breathless.

When I finally pulled in the driveway at Petunia's, I didn't check my phone messages until the engine was off and I was parked. Three missed calls from Crew and half a dozen texts told me he was worried but trying to be patient.

I bypassed Mom and Daisy and hurried down to my apartment, hoping to avoid everyone until I had another solid night of sleep under me. Surely a hot bath and some quiet time and rest would set my mind right. Petunia clattered down the steps behind me, her panting eagerness, it turned out, not aimed at me but at the tall, gorgeous man standing quietly, patiently but with a worried expression on his face, in the center of my kitchen.

CHAPTER THIRTY-FIVE

I didn't give him a chance to ask me where I'd been, instead tackling him and hugging him. He held me without a word for a long moment before guiding me to the sofa and sitting, still holding me. I shifted out of my coat, snuggling into his broad chest and just breathing him in while his steady heartbeat settled my own pounding pulse enough I knew I was going to be okay.

And that I should have told him everything from day one.

So, I did. I started talking and he listened as I dumped everything on him, in random order, knowing I was all over the place and likely sounded like a crazy woman but unable to stop the flood of words and worry that bubbled out. I filled him in on my fears about Rosebert, the news about Siobhan, Vivian's request, my concerns about the Pattersons, about Alicia and Jared and Aundrea and even Pamela. How I knew I'd be hurting my father if I dug up what happened to Fiona Doyle. That I couldn't remember the death of Victor French and that Vivian and I were old friends. On and on, unwinding the coil of anxious partial truths and guestimates I'd been making for what felt like ages now, culminated in that terrible, lonely and self-punishing drive I'd just taken.

When I was done, Petunia had wriggled her way into Crew's lap with her head on my knees where she watched us with her black triangle ears perked as if she understood everything I'd said. Crew waited a good ten seconds after I was done before he sighed, lifting one big hand to touch my chin and tilt my face up toward him. When he kissed me, I felt the very last vestiges of my worry lift, float free and dissolve under the pressure of his delicious lips.

"Fee." He whispered that over my mouth, blue eyes full of the sort of emotions that made my heart go pitter-pat. "It's going to be okay." Had he said that to Jill? Was that why she asked me that question this morning in that particular way? Likely. "We'll figure it out together. Please, let me help you. Let me be your mountain." He kissed me again while I tried to nod and say yes but found it impossible to talk while he gave me that kind of intense attention.

When he finally lifted his mouth from mine, he hugged me, lips pressing to my ear and I realized it was his turn to talk.

"I thought I almost lost you again." Definitely choked up this time. I hugged him back, wishing I could take that fear from him but knowing I'd do it again. Likely would if I knew myself and admitted the truth. Hoped I wouldn't have to, but... yeah. I was a Fleming, after all. "More than ever, nothing matters. Not my job, not politics or the Pattersons or old mysteries. Or pirate treasure." I wanted to protest. It all mattered. But Crew wasn't done. "Just you, Fee. Only you matter to me."

I opened my mouth to speak, silenced by an index finger to my lips, soft, pleading.

"I wanted to do this the other night." He sounded vaguely amused mixed with frustration while he shifted positions, making Petunia moan in protest before she found a new place to get comfy. Meanwhile, the man I loved had something in his hand, something he'd fetched from his front pocket, a small, blue velvet square that made the whole world go away when he offered it to me.

Oh.

My.

God.

"Since dinner that night at the lodge, when I tried to make it perfect, I've tried a bunch of times to spit it out already. To make it special, so you'd know how much I love you." He swallowed while I barely heard him but registered everything he said, as weird as that sounded. "Now I'm thinking maybe our way is this way. Just do it already." He laughed then, taking my shaking hand and pressing the soft box into my trembling fingers, his own not so steady, either.

He had to help me open it because I couldn't breathe and suddenly, I couldn't really see because the world swam in tears I didn't seem able to control. Something sparkly and beautiful cast light through the moisture as I blinked and stared down at the stunningly perfect diamond ring staring back at me.

All while Crew leaned in and whispered in my ear, "Fiona Fleming, will you marry me?"

The Reading Reader Gazette

VOLUME 1   ISSUE 1   MARCH 15TH, 2020   WWW.RRGAZETTE.COM

News Briefs

1. **Junior Detectives Meeting**: Please contact John Fleming at Fleming Investigations OR signup at the front desk at town hall for our new Junior Detectives Club. Parents please note children must be over the age of twelve as consent to visit the morgue must be given.

2. **Parking Violations**: Your town council would like to remind you that parking restrictions continue year round. Any Reading resident caught street parking will be reprimanded and their car impounded. While we realize parking has become a major issue for our town, the sheriff's department is authorized to remove your car without notice. They ask you to please park responsibly and with our town's continuing prosperity in mind. Let's keep Reading's streets safe!

3. **Stolen Mailbox**: Could anyone with information please come forward regarding the specialty pirate treasure chest mailbox gifted to Mayor Olivia Walker. It was expensive and the town paid for it. No questions asked. We just need the mailbox back. Thank you.

4. **Statue Pranks**: We give up. Feel free to decorate Captain Reading however you like. We'll even supply suggestions, if you want. Need fresh paint? Come to the front desk at town hall and we'll supply it. Just please stop using that ugly yellow. It's hideous and we can't stand it anymore. Please? Red's nice. Blue. Purple. Enough with the yellow already.

Winner of this week's Fire Hall 50/50 draw: Jill Wagner. Congratulations, Jill!

Please send any pending community notices to: pamela@rrgazette.com before 4PM.

Dastardly Death by Design(er)

Frederick Newmark, 59, of Queens, NY, is in police custody for the murder of rising modeling star Faith Leeman.

Maligning Model Murder Motivated by Mischief

By Pamela Shard

Death came swiftly to Faith Leeman, 22, of Fort Worth, Texas, an end doled out by aging fashion designer Frederick Newmark of Queens. Once a shining light in the design world, Newmark's fall from grace has led him to imprisonment thanks to his underhanded dealings with both Leeman, his victim, and model Kami Denham. In a web of lies, deceit, drugs and pregnancy, Newmark's endless spiral into criminal activity hit its inevitable conclusion when, faced with blackmail by Leeman, he first stunned her with a stolen weapon and then hung her by the neck with another designer's dress to deflect the blame.

"Miss Leeman's tragic death will be felt throughout the modeling community," says Henry Ostler, Leeman's agent. "Faith's skill and beauty will never be matched and she will be missed."

Yet again the Reading Sheriff's department received invaluable assistance from Fiona Fleming Investigations.

"My daughter's abilities should never come into question," says John Fleming, co-owner of the agency and former sheriff of Reading. "She's proven her mettle time and again and I hope she'll finally be granted the leeway she deserves to assist investigations in the future." As for Miss Fleming, she had this to say:

"No comment."

The continuing bungling of criminal investigations by the sheriff's office has, at this time, shone a light on the devolving control Sheriff Crew Turner seems to have over his deputies. In fact, Deputy Jill Wagner was on the other side of the fence in this case, working privately for the fashion show, a clear break in the command chain.

Says Deputy Robert Carlisle, "One of these days, someone's going to get hurt and it'll be Fanny and Crew's fault."

Considering nine people have been murdered since Crew Turner took over the sheriff's chair, perhaps Deputy Carlisle's comments are a bit late out of the gate.

Mayor Walker refused to comment on the end

278

Looking for more Fiona Fleming? Book ten, *Plaid and Fore! and Murder* is available right now!

AUTHOR NOTES

My very dear reader:

I'm not above admitting I cried and giggled and hugged myself when I wrote that last line. Fee and Crew have become my family, as much as the entire gang in Reading are now an integral part of my life. When I set out to write the first book, I had no idea just how attached I'd become to the trials and hurts they endured over the last nine books, nor the absolute satisfaction I felt being able to finally put these two people together.

While I've never been a romance writer, I am a soggy, weepy mess when people I love find one another, imaginary characters or not. It's been a long time coming for them, and I can't be happier to put two people's paths into sync than them.

Okay, enough of the gushy stuff, right? I've had so many of you ask me if I'm really stopping at thirteen books to which I honestly have to shrug and tell you, "Maybe." Like many of my characters, Fee is headstrong, opinionated and has her own way of doing things that is beyond my ken. She's already whispered about further volumes, though I have, as yet, to receive instructions past book thirteen. And, in case you missed it, there was a pretty blatant foreshadowing for a spinoff series starring Alice Moore and Denver Hatch. So we'll be seeing Fee again, though from another perspective.

Meanwhile, I'm already at work on book ten,

Plaid and Fore! and Murder. These last few books have come slowly, with months between, and I'm sorry for the delays. My own romance has come to an end and I'm finding myself again, sometimes in the pages of my own books and sometimes in the real world, out there where I am reconnecting with the woman I thought I'd only imagined I could be.

As always, happy reading.

Best,

Patti

ABOUT THE AUTHOR

EVERYTHING YOU NEED TO know about me is in this one statement: I've wanted to be a writer since I was a little girl, and now I'm doing it. How cool is that, being able to follow your dream and make it reality? I've tried everything from university to college, graduating the second with a journalism diploma (I sucked at telling real stories), am an enthusiastic member of an all-girl improv troupe (if you've never tried it, I highly recommend making things up as you go along as often as possible) and I get to teach and perform with an amazing group of women I adore. I've even been in a Celtic girl band (some of our stuff is on YouTube!) and was an independent film maker (go check out the Lovely Witches Club at www.lovelywitchesclub.com). My life has been one creative thing after another—all leading me here, to writing books for a living.

Now with multiple series in happy publication, I live on beautiful and magical Prince Edward Island (I know you've heard of Anne of Green Gables) with my multitude of pets.

I love-love-love hearing from you! You can reach me (and I promise I'll message back) at patti@pattilarsen.com. And if you're eager for your next dose of Patti Larsen books (usually about one release a month) come join my mailing list! All the best up and coming, giveaways, contests and, of course, my observations on the world (aren't you just dying to know what I think about everything?) all in one place: http://bit.ly/PattiLarsenEmail.

Last—but not least!—I hope you enjoyed what you read! Your happiness is my happiness. And I'd love to hear just what you thought. A review where you found this book would mean the world to me— reviews feed writers more than you will ever know. So, loved it (or not so much), your honest review would make my day. Thank you!

Made in United States
North Haven, CT
29 August 2024

56708160R00157